Beyond the
Good & Evil

Francisco Dosal

Urban Book Publisher
a division of Urban Book Editor LLC
PO Box 390665
Snellville, GA 30039

Beyond the Good & Evil

ISBN(10): 0-9861519-3-9

ISBN(13): 978-0-9861519-3-4

This book is a work of fiction. Names, characters, places, and incidents are products of the author's imagination or are used fictitiously. Any resemblance to actual events or locales or persons, living or dead, is entirely coincidental.

Book cover design by Abdul Walker.

Printed in the United States.

I would like to thank and dedicate my first novel to my parents – my mother, who when I told her I was writing a story told me to write something beautiful; my father, who without knowing is a great story teller. Second, the readers who spent their time and money to read my book. Finally, to the very few who believed in me.

Beyond the
Good & Evil

Table of Contents

January 13, 2006

Please forgive me, but you need something better than a black and white composition book. Or you can use this to write down your dreams, or your nightmares or your ideas, or your songs, or your visions of the future. Write about your family in Mexico. Write about coming to the United States. Write about four years ago. Write about four months ago. Write about everything!

I don't know if we're born or we grow the desire to look into the future and hope for a better tomorrow. All I know is before that night I had never dreamed of my fate. As far as I was concerned, that didn't matter. Feeling my demise approach, I daydreamed of what could have been for the first time. I looked at the moon and contemplated if it was really up there. I've always had the idea that the floating rock didn't exist unless I was looking at it. I thought about myself and questioned if I was real. I could see everyone's faces but mine. So how could I prove my own being?

Looking up at the glittering stars, I searched the universe as if proof of my own existence would be found there. Nothing. Hopeless, I watched the sun crawl from darkness as I reached for my rosary and tightly held on to the wooden cross on it. My numb skin waited eagerly for its warm rays. A morning breeze lifted sand into the air and made its way toward me. As the sun climbed higher and grew brighter, I felt transparent like air. I wondered if this was what death felt like. Scared, I closed my eyes trying to replay my short life like some sort of film. Searching for something to justify my entrance to heaven. Violence, murder, and evil flashed before my eyes. I gave my half smile thinking, *hell can't be that bad.* If I had the energy, I would have cried. It was unfair that from the moment of my birth I was given no choice of the kind of life I wanted to live. Being born into a barbaric and cruel life, I had no other dream but to survive. Now, I was on the verge of losing my chance to leave everything behind and create my own vision of the kind of man I wanted to be. For the first time, I feared death.

***

One morning, before the sun rose, I led the sheep into the valley and left them. When I returned home, my two older brothers were feeding the horses. Luis looked at me. I thought about starting a conversation, but nothing came to mind. I lowered my head and made my way to Fabian, who was busy taming Don Felipe's wild horse. I could tell he had made some progress because Fabian finally strapped the saddle onto the horse.

"Oye, Fabian," I yelled. "Me lo prestas?" I waited for his response on whether I could mount the horse or not.

"No," he said brushing his hand down the horse's thigh. The door swung open.

"Vengan," our father ordered us inside. Looking down, I ignored his overpowering brown eyes and wondered if he knew.

We all sat around the kitchen table except our father. I was scared as to what he called us in for.

"Vamonos pa America, Alejandro," he stared.

"Vamos," Luis and Fabian agreed.

"Las cosas están saliendo de control aquí," my father said.

"Que pues, Alejandro?" Luis asked me. I thought about what my father said. Everything came into focus. After the murder of Pablo Enerma and his son, we had to leave. Glancing at the kitchen sink

10

where my mother would usually be humming a sweet lullaby, I knew either way our lives weren't going to be the same anymore. No one knew what I had done and I wanted to keep it that way.

Our first day towards the Arizona border was bearable. Walking in the desert was nothing new to me or for the rest of the group I was traveling with, unlike Hugo. He'd only brought two gallons of water and no winter jacket as if he were out for a short hike. I could only assume he was a city boy, maybe from Mexico City. I never did trust anyone from Mexico City.

"Mama!" a small child cried to his mother. I looked at him as the pale moonlight shined down on his scared face. Holding his mother's hand, he cried and complained about having been walking all day with little to no rest. I tried ignoring him, but his whining was unbearable. I occasionally looked at the mother expecting her to respond in some way, but she never did. She just tuned him out, which was something I couldn't do. Perhaps she thought that he'd just run out of energy. He never did. It wasn't long before she gave up and struck him in the face. Telling him that he'd better not cry, or she'd hit him again. He just stared at his mother with a distorted face on the verge of tears.

"Pinche madre, está frío, no!" Hugo said wrapping his hands around his freezing body. No one responded or even offered their jacket as he had hoped for.

Hugo died on his third day in the desert. I had been trying to find a comfortable spot to rest, but everywhere I turned a rock would stab me in the spine or the rib cage and just as I was ready to close my eyes, it was time to get moving again. Everyone slowly and painfully got to their feet except one. Hugo lay on the ground motionless as a rock. I nudged him, hoping he was in a deep sleep.

"El que puede, puede. Y el que no. Que Dios le ayude," Fabian said.

Examining Hugo's body, I didn't think anything of his death because like my brother said, those who can, can. And those who can't, may God help them. Everyone dies. I had known that from a young age. Thoughts of my own demise had never bothered me because no matter how I decided to live my life, death was the only thing waiting for me and everyone else.

***

"Por favor," I whispered. I squeezed my rosary tighter and wondered how long I had been in this wasteland. The sun had completely risen, but my skin still felt cold. The desert sand continued pushing towards me. I could see the wind and dirt crash into my face but never felt it. I began to feel my body being lifted. I tried to imagine a life where I had a choice. I saw myself in a classroom with a book resting on my shoulder. I searched the horizon for the moon. If I died, would we both cease to exist? Would we both be lost? Then, I understood. "Por favor," I pleaded once more and the urge to survive quickly grew within me.

Chapter I

The door swung open. Her heels clicked against the hardwood floor as she made her way to the bar. All the men, and even the few women in the bar, turned to look at her. She wore a black dress tightly wrapped around her caramel skin. Chocolate brown eyes hid behind her long, curly bangs. When she noticed everyone appraising her, a slight grin appeared on her face. *Tonight is going to be another great night out!* she thought.

Persela majestically sat down on the bar stool next to a man. He did not bother to look at her or introduce himself, which bothered her a little. She leaned over the bar and began examining the alcohol on the display shelves. Overhead lights shined onto the bottles. Their glimmering reflections screamed out to her. Attempting to restrain her joy from bursting out uncontrollably, she bit her lower lip. *A shot of whiskey*, she thought. *No, a shot of tequila!* She argued with herself. Scanning the wide variety of alcohol, her excitement only grew. Persela giggled inside like a child in a candy shop. *I know!* she thought. *I'll start with a shot of rum.* She reached towards her right hip where her purse usually rested. Not finding it, she recalled her mission.

Like a spy secretly identifying his target, Persela used the large mirror that stood behind the display shelves to stealthily check out the man sitting next to her. He was looking straight ahead. He picked up his shot glass of what looked like vodka and raised it to his lips. He stopped as if hesitating to take a drink. Persela waited for him to glance over at her. She needed to know he had the least bit of interest in her, but he never looked her way. She took in his expensive, tailored black suit and matching gloves. Diamond cufflinks shone brightly on each wrist. He was a good-looking man. His high cheekbones gave him an aristocratic look and at the same time made him look intimidating. He had straight eyebrows that rested above penetrating dark brown eyes.

Persela struggled to think of something to say. She looked back at his eyes expecting to catch him adoring her, but he was not. Slowly, the man tilted his head back. The liquid must have burned down his throat, but his face remained calm. After he finished his drink, he continued to hold the glass near his lips. *He will have to look at me now*, she thought.

"It is not polite to stare." His voice was gentle yet the sentiment was heavy.

Persela's eyes turned elsewhere as her caramel cheeks blushed pink with embarrassment. Not knowing how to respond or whether to respond at all, she pretended to have not heard him. Convincing herself that she was being wrongfully accused, she began flickering her fingers. Her lips were ready to reply with a smart comment when she realized, *he had been admiring me this whole time.*

"So, what's your name?" he asked.

"Persela," she smiled and lightly laughed.

"Per, Se, La," he repeated, emphasizing every syllable in her name.

Persela felt like she was being studied now. Her rosy pink cheeks vanished from her face. Her natural beautiful brown skin reappeared. "What about yours?" she asked enthusiastically. This was her opportunity; she was going in for the kill. The man raised his right arm in the air and waved, signaling the bartender to pour him another shot.

More interested in receiving his next shot than Persela's question, he did not reply. Persela was focused on her prey so she patiently waited to hear his name. He looked at her and she smiled. *I've got him*, she thought. He looked away again, but it was already too late according to Persela. She had won the moment he turned to acknowledge her. He turned back towards her. His piercing brown eyes penetrated through her bangs and stared into her eyes. She froze as she was now the center of his attention. Her lips trembled and her fingers fiddled with her dress. She panicked not knowing what to say or do. Persela was ready to turn her attention elsewhere until a smile appeared on his face. It was a childish kind of smile, yet it seemed to tell Persela more than his name ever could. He seemed trustworthy, generous, and filled with life. She leaned closer to him and smiled back. She found herself attracted to the mysterious man. Stumbling with words, she tried asking for his name again but could not.

"I come here whenever I get a chance," he said. His eyes stayed fixed on Persela. "What brings you here? Persela," he said softly.

Remembering why she was there, Persela replied, "Maybe if you buy me a drink, I'll tell you, honey." In Persela's mind all men, rich, poor, ugly or handsome, thought the same. What man in his right mind would deny her? Persela knew that even though this man did not show a serious interest towards her, he wanted her. All she needed to do was tease him a little. She looked back at the man with seductive eyes. Biting her lower lip, she slightly opened her legs.

Disgusted, his smile disappeared.

"Sorry, I'm not that kind of guy," he said as the bartender finally poured him another shot. He turned his attention away from Persela and resumed his previous stance, staring into space. "Perhaps some other guy will gladly buy you a drink. You are a very gorgeous young woman," he explained. He looked down at his drink and then started searching inside his blazer jacket. Finding his wallet, he picked through some bills.

Persela was shocked and puzzled at what had just happened. For the first time in her life, she had been rejected. She wondered why this man refused to buy her a drink. Her confusion transformed into anger that a low life man in a low life bar refused to purchase her a drink even after she opened her legs like some whore. She felt the need to explain that she was not that type of girl but was disgusted at the idea of having to explain herself to this scum. She knew she was not that type of girl and only did it because guys in bars fell for stuff like that. Furious, she closed her legs and turned her body away from him. *I'm not that kind of guy.* The words played over and over inside her head. She could hear him getting up from his seat. She did not bother to look at him and say goodbye.

What a dick, Persela thought as she turned to watch him leave. Her face skipped pink and turned red. When he exited the bar and darkness embraced him, her anger and puzzlement left with him. Relaxed and at ease once more, she turned her attention back to the bar where she noticed the man had left his ordered shot untouched.

Persela looked at the glass, not knowing whether to take the shot or not. *Did he leave it for me or did he do it on accident?* she thought. She wondered if the man was playing the same mind game she had intended on winning. She wanted to drink it, but if she did she would lose the game they were secretly playing. She decided against it.

Alone, a man made his way towards Persela. He was a lot older than the first one. He had wrinkled loose skin that rested on his face and yellow teeth that suggested he smoked constantly or never found the time for personal hygiene.

"Can I offer you somethin' to drink?" he said with a rusty voice and a devilish smirk. Persela responded with a flirtatious smile and accepted. "Ma name's Chuck, by the way."

"What a gentleman you are, Chuck," Persela said smiling.

After a couple shots, two younger men joined them. Persela could not decide which one was more attractive as Gary was a dirty blonde and Robert a brunette. *Maybe if Gary was a complete blonde*, she thought.

"Gosh, you the prettiest girl I done ever seen. You know that? Hey! Can we get this pretty little thang another drink?" Robert yelled.

"Yea, come on now!" Gary agreed.

"I ain't never seen a girl like you," Robert explained.

"Oh, my God, thank you!" Persela replied. "You guys are the nicest. We need to hand out more."

"You know, we're leaving pretty soon," said Robert as he took out his phone, looking at the time.

"Yea, you should join us back to our place," suggested Gary as he reached over and caressed Persela's hand. "You know you can trust us baby girl. We gonna have fun." That's when Persela's phone began to vibrate. She gently pulled her hand away from Gary and reached inside her bra. It was a sight the men could not ignore. The three glanced at each other competitively. When they looked away from each other, they saw Persela texting on her phone. As she finished, they watched her slide her phone down her chest and into her bra. How they wished they could have been that phone that very moment.

"Where's the restroom?" Persela asked with ease as she caught them looking at her breast. Gary pointed as Robert explained where it was. Chuck said nothing, instead he stared at Persela with a devilish smirk. "I'll be back," she said with a flirtatious smile. "Don't go anywhere."

Walking towards the restroom, she looked for the untouched drink the earlier man had left behind. His black gloves then came to mind. She wondered why he wore them. *He's probably an assassin who after finishing every job comes to drink his guilt away.* She laughed at her imagination. As Persela neared the restroom, she glanced back toward the men and noticed them arguing with one another. Robert jammed his finger deep into Gary's chest and then he pointed at himself as if claiming ownership. Persela could only imagine what they were arguing about, but she had a good idea it involved her. A glass fell over and broke. This was her chance. Persela stepped out the bar without being seen and into the back alley.

"Persela!" yelled a familiar voice, "over here!"

17

The drinks had made everything foggy.

"Over here!" yelled the voice again.

Persela noticed a blue car with hands waving out of the driver's window. The driver stepped out. The young woman was tall and slim. She wore a blue dress that was just as short as Persela's. She had straight dark black hair that only came down to her shoulders and having no bangs, her hazel eyes shone in the dark night.

"Helene!" yelled Persela in her energetic and bubbly tone. Helene responded by yelling out Persela's name with the same tone and attitude. "I got your text and, oh, my God, did you do it at the right time!" The passenger and back doors opened. "Anthony! Josh!" Persela shouted.

Josh was a tall, handsome man with a muscular body structure and dreadlocks that came down to his neck. He carried a strong, serious face and composure that matched his physic. Unlike Anthony, who was smaller than Josh and had a more relaxed personality.

"Come on Persela, get the fuck in," Anthony demanded. Approaching her, he kissed her soft lips. He ran his tongue around her lips and tasted liquor. "You're cheating. You know you're not allowed to start without us," Anthony said as he picked Persela up. Tossing her over his shoulder, he carried her to the car. Before throwing her in the car, he spanked her thigh. "Let's go, Helene!" Anthony shouted.

"You guys are so cute together," Helene pouted.

Chapter II

October 12, 2010
My mind is a bit blurry as it tends to skip around

All the alcohol and drugs had me in a motionless trance. I just stood there blankly staring at the fire twirling and twisting in the air. Sweat poured off my face. I could feel my body trying to push me away from the flames, but I remained motionless. My body vibrated with my heart's steady beat.

I looked at the fire, and everything seemed to come back into existence. Like an image rendering on a computer screen, a forest reappeared from behind the flames and groups of people were scattered everywhere. I was at a bonfire, a party celebrating our freshman year in high school. With all the empty cans of beer on the ground, it looked like a storm had blown through.

"What the fuck am I doing with my life?" I whispered to the flames.

My tongue slid around my lips to find them dry. I raised my plastic cup. Empty. I sighed at the thought of having to refill it. I looked around until my eyes found a keg nearby. Stumbling, I escaped the bonfire's heat. My body was unprepared for the bitter night air. My muscles tightened and every bone shivered uncontrollably. Wrapping my arms around myself, I noticed a couple. Watching them disappear into the forest, I reached the keg. My phone buzzed. I ignored it. Refilling my cup was far more important than a phone call. I witnessed as another couple disappear into the woods. I pondered if what I was seeing was love, actual love. It had to be. The couple had stared into each other's eyes before disappearing into the darkness. *It has to be*, I thought. I felt envy inside my heart. I wanted to look into someone's eyes the way they had.

I turned away from the lovers and toward the keg. My hand tried to reach for it, but it seemed to get farther and farther away. Afraid of what was happening, I crumbled onto the ground. My ringtone went off again. My body was heavy, but I managed to lift my head. I was dizzy and everything was foggy. A sharp pain grew in my stomach as if my intestines were being tied into knots. I laid back down and a cold chill ran up my spine as I felt something wet on my shoulder. It had a strong acidic smell, kind of like ammonia.

"What the fuck am I doing with my life?" My eyes wandered with no direction. A glittering light shined above me. I looked up searching for the moon but couldn't find it. I was lost and, because of that, so was the moon.

I heard my phone buzz for the third time. I struggled but managed to successfully free it from my pocket. The voice on the other end yelled something at me, "Dude, COPS!"

"What?"

"COPS!"

"COPS!" I yelled and stumbled to my feet.

Everyone panicked and started running around chaotically. I bolted into the forest. Someone ran past me. I looked over at him and he looked like he was choking on something. He stopped and vomited all over his shirt before falling to his knees. I jerked away from him and bumped into a couple. They were half-naked and desperately trying to put their clothes back on. They tried to run and clothe themselves at the same time but only tripped and fell behind me. I heard the girl cry out for help. It was too late. I couldn't turn back now. Someone else crossed my path, he was covering his private parts with his hands as he made his way back to the campfire. He yelled out someone's name. His name was yelled in reply. The name calling faded the farther I went into the dark woods. Something landed on my face and scratched me. I pushed through bushes and tree branches. It was impossible to see if I was bleeding or sweating, but I knew the smell of blood. The copper scent crawled up my nostrils and my face twitched.

***

It had been nearly four years since the last time the smell of blood went up my nose. I was ten years old at the time. I was smoking a Cuban cigar with Tito and five others around a pool table. I grabbed a pool stick and set up the table. That's when Tito lost his cool.

"Chinga Nico," he said.

The idea of killing Nico was a good idea. I didn't say anything, I just glanced at Tito and shrugged my shoulders. I cocked my hand back ready to break when my left shoulder was hit. I fell to the ground as the place became a shooting range. My face twitched as the smell of copper filled the room.

***

Enraged that my face was getting a nonstop beating, I waved my hands as if I was being attacked by a swarm of bees. Just then, I hit open space. I panicked and tried to catch my footing, but it was too late. I fell over and landed on my face. I grunted in pain. Blood and sweat came down my cheek bone and into my mouth. I spat it out and tried to wipe my face clean.

"Brother, is that you?" whispered a voice from the dark. I recognized the country voice and knew it was Grant.

"Yea," I grunted in agony.

"Brother, it's me. Grant and de rest," he whispered. I wondered what he meant by "the rest." I didn't bother to ask. I laid there trying to think of a way to get out of there. I wanted to go home. I wanted to be in a comfortable bed not having to worry about getting into trouble, but it was too late. I was already here. I was beginning to

21

regret the freshman bonfire. I got up when Grant called my name again. He came out from the woods and so did others. Grant was wearing a trench coat that stretched from his shoulders all the way to his feet. He looked like someone from a detective movie. I looked behind Grant. Their faces were somewhat hidden, but I saw at least a dozen. I scanned all them trying to find recognizable faces, but didn't.

"Brother, we gotta get de fuck outta here before we get caught and arrested," Grant explained. He frantically looked in every direction making sure nothing would sneak up from behind a tree. He was beginning to worry me. Grant always kept his composure in difficult situations. It may have been the alcohol or drugs that caused him to lose focus, but he sounded worried. I could hear it in his voice. Grant looked at me again.

"Brother, I'm still fucked up. I can barely walk, let alone run from cops. I mean where can we go?" I asked. Grant continued looking at me.

"Wait, you guys are brothers?" whispered a voice from the group. I wanted to say something but wasn't willing to risk getting caught for such a stupid question. With no light around, no one could see that Grant was clearly darker than me.

A flashlight shined on a tree then all around us. We ducked just in time. Silence took over. No one said anything. I felt the blood vessel in my neck pumping. I swallowed some saliva to ease the tension in my throat. I felt lightheaded. Blood and sweat slowly ran down my face. It tingled, but I refused to make any sudden movements. I looked over to where the light had come from. Bushes started moving. A tree branch snapped close to where we were. Whoever or whatever was out there, was getting closer. Grant's eyes widened as he heard another snap. The noises stopped.

"We gotta make it to de abandoned house. We can stay da night there. You know it ain't safe out here, brother," Grant whispered. No one said anything, not that they wanted to. No one knew how to feel about the plan. We exchanged glances at one another.

"We have to make a run for it. Spread out in different directions, brother," I finally suggested. "If we're in a group it'll be easier for them to catch us all together rather than making it difficult for them by scattering."

"Put your hands in the air!" yelled a voice so deep it shook my vision. I turned around. A light shined on my face. Blinded, I froze. My heart fell into my stomach, and I had the urge to puke. The officer was staring at all of us. He began to slowly lift his right foot to move in closer. Everyone stayed still. His right foot descended and landed on a branch. Crack! Everyone scattered.

I ran as fast as I could while leaping over logs and dodging branches. I ran left, then right, and then left again. I thought that maybe if I ran in random directions, with no pattern, the cops could not predict in what direction I would go. I probably looked like a maniac escaping a penitentiary, but I needed to escape. But escape to where? That's when I considered the abandoned house. I sprinted when I found the trail that led to the safe house. Bolting down the trail, I felt like an easy target on an open field. I ran faster than before hoping to reach the house before anyone would notice me. A sharp pain grew inside my chest. I wanted to stop. I wanted to catch my breath and rest for a minute, but I knew that decision could define my fate. I had to push through it until I reached my destination or, at least, jump over the fence that surrounded the house.

Ahead, a flashlight was being pointed at a figure. I stopped and hunched down. The flashlight shined brightly on a trench coat. I stopped breathing completely, hoping the cop would not spot me. It didn't take long for the cop to catch up to Grant. Grant leapt to jump over a log when the cop reached over and grabbed his trench coat. Grant fell backwards. He coughed in pain when he hit the ground. The officer pulled out his gun and pointed it at him. As Grant lay on his back, he slowly put his hands above his head. He made no attempt to run. I couldn't let this happen. I needed to do something, but what would I do? He had a gun and I didn't.

I saw a thick tree branch. I grabbed it and tightly wrapped my hands around it. I sprinted towards them and just as the cop was turning Grant over, I swung the tree branch at his face. The cop flew off Grant before he could cuff him. The officer's flashlight flew into the air. It landed on the ground and shined onto his motionless body. I grabbed the officer's gun and tucked it into my pants. Then, I quickly checked his pulse. He seemed to be alive. I wasn't sure though. I placed my ear on his mouth and thought I could feel and hear him breathing.

"What the fuck were you thinkin'?" Grant asked in disbelief.

"I guess nothing," I replied. "I couldn't let that happen."

"We gotta get to the house before he," another noise came from the woods causing Grant to stop mid-sentence. We froze like deer. The bushes moved closer towards us. I reached for the gun as a wild half-naked beast appeared. He ran past us sprinting toward the path to the house when he suddenly stopped. He was short with tattoos all over his body. We stared at him attempting to discover who he was.

"Oreo," Grant said with a laugh. "what in de hell happen to you?"

"We need," Oreo said and then paused to catch his breath, "to get to the fuckin' house." He sounded like a fish out of water. "Cops are all over. I barely made it out. I had to leave… my girlfriend, dude…that's how you know it's serious."

The abandoned wooden house was two stories high with a garage and a porch that wrapped around the house. It sat in the middle of nowhere on private property, hidden deep in the woods. Resting on top of a hill, it gave an amazing view of the surrounding area. It was a great view to spot game or cops. The prior occupant had made sure to board up the house. Not a window or door was left open. Luckily, the garage door was left unlocked and could easily be lifted. It was a perfect place for us to take over and make a home away from home.

24

We walked towards the garage door. Grant lifted it open so Oreo and I would crawl inside. We did the same for him. Down in the basement, we heard whispering. Oreo entered first.

"Hope!" Oreo cried awkwardly. His voice cracked a bit.

Grant and I followed him to see Hope and another girl cowered together. Hope was a petite girl with straight brunette hair that came down to her lower back and bright blue eyes. A gentle smile grew on my face. Hope seemed to brighten the house more than a flashlight or lamp ever could. The other girl had dirty-blonde hair and a thick body. She wore jeans that tightly wrapped her heavy thighs and an oversized shirt that hung loosely on her shoulders.

"Babe, I'm so glad you're ok," Hope said sounding concerned. She jumped onto Oreo wrapping her arms and legs around him. "I was so worried when you didn't come back. Delilah found me and told me everyone was headed here." Oreo was speechless. How could he explain he had left her behind with no intentions of returning for her? Grant and I looked at each other and laughed. I knew he had left Hope in the middle of sex after hearing that the cops had crashed the party. He probably told Hope he would be back as soon as he found help, which I knew was a lie. Why would he need help? "Ain't no bitch worth getting arrested for," he once explained to me. Although I completely disagreed, I had simply nodded my head. "I just knew you were gonna be here, well Delilah did. You know I was waiting for you when Delilah found me. I told her I wasn't gonna leave but she promised me you would be here. Baby, I'm so glad you're here. I don't know what I would have done without you. Oh, Ally and Grant, this is Delilah." Hope pointed towards the girl I had just been admiring. "Oh, my baby is ok! Baby. Baby. My baby."

"So, this party was a bust!" Oreo started when we all settled in. "You know I knew it from the very get go. But whatever. I knew that old lady was gonna say some shit. Just by the way she looked at us. She knew we were up to something. I fuckn' hate cops man. Really. Like do we really need them?" Hope repeatedly glanced at me, expecting me to give my opinion every time Oreo made a statement, but I didn't feel like debating. "It's society man," Oreo said.

"Yea," Hope agreed as she wrapped her arms around him.

"Yea. I just want to live like this forever. Just happy, with you guys. Smoking and drinking and sleeping. No more problems. No more war," Oreo explained. He began to explain in more detail of what he meant, but I was barely listening. When my attention returned to Oreo, he was explaining how much he hated school. "I'm skipping first period Monday and going to the T.P. if anyone wants to come along." No one besides Hope raised their hand. I couldn't help but feel worried. I thought about saying something but, I kept my mouth closed. I didn't want Oreo to accuse me of being jealous. I just hoped nothing bad came out of all this. I really did care for Hope. For the first time in my life, someone actually cared about me without reason. She was my first actual friend.

"So, whatever happened to Nico? You never finished your story from earlier today, brother," Grant asked trying to change the subject. The bright moonlight finally reappeared in the sky and pierced through a small window. I could see everyone looking at me besides Hope, who had fallen asleep on Oreo's shoulder.

"I killed him," I stated.

"Brother, come on, really? What happen'?" Grant protested. "You were ten."

"Yea. I mean, I guess" was all I could reply. "It's normal over there. People die all the time, brother."

"That's crazy," Grant said.

"Yea, if it's one thing I learned is that what is normal here isn't normal over there."

"Like what?" Grant asked.

"From a young age and maybe ever since I can remember I'm used to seeing things die. I remember seeing my father running a knife into a pig and all sorts of animals," I said with a wry smile. I grabbed the gun from behind me and placed it on the floor next to me. Everyone flinched except Delilah. Her eyes widened in excitement.

"So, how'd you kill 'em, brother?" Grant asked curiously.

"I walked up behind him one day, stuck a blade in his neck, and slid his throat wide open."

"Brother," Grant said in disbelief. "I don't believe you. At age ten!" Grant stared at me. I could tell he was trying to figure out if I was telling the truth or not. "How old was he? You ever done somethin' like that before?"

"I think fifteen. And, yea, plenty of animals, you know. Like when I would go hunting with my brothers."

"Yea, huntin', brother," Grant said.

Thinking back, I don't recall flinching or thinking twice about what I did to Nico. I just reached over his neck and in a couple of seconds it was over. He laid on the floor trying to hold his throat together. It was pointless. In a moment, he would bleed to death. He tried screaming but couldn't. Hearing his last breath come out of his lungs, I looked down at the knife and for a split second, thought about killing myself. I thought about how maybe I'd be doing the world a favor, but it occurred to me that Nico would have done it to me if I hadn't done it to him first. "Were animals Grant. All capable of killing," I muttered under my breath.

"You didn't get caught? Wait? You weren't in school?" Oreo asked.

"No. I'm not dumb. And, I mean, no one has time for school. We had to care for the animals and tend the fields. And our lives."

"Man, I could live with that," Oreo said smacking his hands together. "Besides the lives part."

"I mean everyone's real old-fashioned and country." I stopped speaking and glanced at Delilah. "Anyways, let's talk about something different. Remember that one kid that bullied me in 6th grade when I first moved here?"

"Yea, big tall white kid. The one that failed twice?"

"Yea, so one day in school I follow him into the bathroom. You know how you can push the back of someone's knee caps and it makes them fall?" I stopped talking and reimagined what happened that day.

***

I had watched his footsteps carefully studying his pace, right foot, left foot. I synchronized my pace with his so he wouldn't be able to hear me as I got close to him. When his left foot rose and his entire body weight rested on his right foot, I kicked the back of his knee. He tumbled, and before he could look back, my right hand was tightly wrapped around his neck. He jerked but thought twice when I reached over with my left hand and pointed my pocket knife straight at him.

***

"Well, one day I kicked the shit out of his leg," I said as Grant started to laugh.

"What did he do?" Grant asked.

"Well, I ran before he could do anything," I lied.

"Yea! Well, he was a dick to everyone. At least you stood up for yourself," Grant said. "He did stop bullyin' you. Didn't he?"

"Yea, he did," I said.

I had the urge to explain that I didn't want that kid to stop bullying me or anyone else. I honestly respected him and his desire to control others through fear and intimidation. In a weird kind of way, it reminded me of home so I didn't mind him bullying me with words. I knew he felt a sense of purpose and meaning making everyone afraid of him. It wasn't until he laid his hands on me that I had to do something.

***

"Pinche perro," I said as I held my pocket knife near his face. "No! No me touch! Oh, te corto tu garganta como el pinch perro de

Nico!" I ran my knife down toward his throat. "No me touch." I gently caressed his throat with my knife before releasing him. "Forget. Ok? Friends." He just shook his head.

I was on guard for a week wondering if he had stopped bullying others so he could plot against me. I walked everywhere, through the hallways and back home, with my right hand inside my pocket gripping my knife. But he never did anything. Instead, he completely stopped bothering me. Whenever he would see me in the hallway, he would turn around and take another route and every time I turned up as he was pushing someone around or was insulting someone, he would stop and leave. I couldn't tell if he was afraid of me or just lost his focus whenever he saw me, but I felt bad for having done what I did. That was the last time I ever did anything like that again. I realized I no longer had to live in fear for my life. Everyone here was all talk and no show. I had learned that whenever a fight broke out, it was only to gain attention.

***

I looked back at Hope's friend, trying to figure out how to include her in the conversation. I had always been awkward around girls. I was not quite the ladies' man like Oreo was. Oreo was smooth and charming. He could have any girl he wanted. He was adored in school because of his confidence. I'd be confident too if I came from a family made of money. I was the complete opposite. I wanted to be the ladies' man. Instead, I was awkward and could never find the right words and, on top of all that, I came from a poor, illegal family. I envied Oreo. I thought about what Oreo might say, "Hey, wanna go to my lake house?" I gave up.

"I'm cold," Delilah whispered as she caught me staring at her. She spoke like an angel, with a serene tone. She seemed hopeless as she sat curled in the cold, waiting for someone to provide the comfort and warmth she needed.

I didn't know how to respond. "Get a blanket," I said knowing there were none in the room. I bit my lower lip to prevent myself from saying anything more humiliating. Delilah giggled as if the comment was meant as a joke.

"You think just for the night...," she started. She seemed to be debating whether to finish her sentence or not. "You think for the night I can sleep with you?"

I froze at her words. I did not know how to respond to her offer. A slight shiver passed over me. *Was I cold or scared of sleeping with such a beautiful girl?* I wondered. I had barely met her and yet she suggested cuddling as if we had been friends for a long time.

"Yea," I finally said as my teeth chattered. She crawled towards me. I could see her cleavage as she seductively made her way towards me like a lioness. Her eyes had the kind of fire that boiled blood. She stretched her arms and pressed her thick warm body against mine. *Was she really cold?* I wondered. She looked into my eyes. They seemed to say, *I know you want me.*

Delilah seemed to know what she was doing, but I didn't. I held her awkwardly. I wondered if she could tell that I was a virgin. She forcefully yet tenderly kissing my lips. Though she tasted blood and felt my busted lip, it didn't seem to bother her. Once our lips met, I found myself doing whatever felt natural. I held her close as my hands explored her body and my tongue explored her mouth.

"I want you," she said softly into my ear. Delilah looked at me, and then at the door. I wanted her just as much as she wanted me, if not more. I had never felt the soft skin of a woman before. I grabbed Delilah by her hand and led her into the next empty room. She closed the door behind her and began ripping her clothes as if she had caught fire. Besides pornography on the internet, I had never seen an actual naked woman before. Now I understood why so many of my friends were transfixed on the opposite sex. She had something I could not explain.

As Delilah rid herself of her clothing, I noticed I still had my own on; I had practically been drooling over her like a creep. She thought it was cute and rather funny. Embarrassed, I rushed to take my clothes off and successfully managed to tangle myself in my shirt and pants. She walked over and freed me. We stood naked together for a minute and stared into one another's eyes. She pressed her hand against my chest, suggesting I lie on my back. As she descended upon me, my heart began to race.

"I love you," I whispered.

Chapter III

"Have some of this," Anthony suggested as he pulled a small, tightly-wrapped, plastic package from his pocket. He tossed it into Persela's palm.

"What it is?" She squeezed it. It didn't break. She tipped her head to the side, trying to take a closer look. "Is it candy?"

"Am I bleeding?" Josh turned to face Anthony. He tipped his head back, "I think I'm bleeding," he said laughing.

"Nah," Anthony replied as he glanced up Josh's nose.

"Goddamn, Persela, how much longer you gonna stare at it?" Josh shouted.

"It'll make you feel good," Anthony said then laughed at what he said. "Come on. You know I wouldn't give you anything I wouldn't do."

Josh snatched the plastic package from Persela's hand and broke what was inside into powder. "Lick your finger. Dip it in and just get a little bit. Just a little bit. I don't think you weigh more than I do. So, you won't need as much."

She did just that. Licking the powder, her face scrunched up.

"Miiiieeee turn!" shouted Helene stepping out of the car. "I need something that'll sober me up after such a long night drinking and clubbing" She reached inside Josh's pocket and took out a small bag filled with cocaine. "Let me see your keys babe." Josh handed them over. Taking a bump of cocaine, her head jerked back as if some invisible force came rushing through her, "Hmmmmmm. Wow. Wow. Who's your plug, baby?"

"The Pool Table Club," Anthony answered for Josh. Helene did not seem to understand. She stared at Anthony blankly then at Josh waiting for an explanation.

"It's nothing, Helene." He snatched his keys and the coke and shoved everything back in his pocket. "It's nothing."

"Yea, it's nothing. You good to drive or you want me to?" Anthony asked trying change the topic. For a quick second, Anthony couldn't help but feel embarrassed that he had made such a stupid mistake. He looked up at Josh, who didn't look worried, and then at Helene, who was already inside her car.

As they drove through the city, Persela began to feel something strange in her mind and body. Having been drunk before, she knew what it was like to be intoxicated, but now she felt like something was crawling up her skin. It started at the tip of her fingers and made its way up her arms. She couldn't help but squirm around in excitement. A sense of warmth took over her body; she tried to resist touching herself but it was impossible. She ran her hands down her thighs. A cold breeze blew down her neck. A tingling jolt ran down her spine and her body was filled with a sensation she did not understand. Persela closed her eyes as her body began to reach a climax she had never had before. Slowly music reached her ears. It began to get louder and louder. She couldn't quite hear the music or understand the lyrics, but she felt it. She opened her eyes. Beautiful colors from all over seemed to jump out at her. Persela giggled. She stretched her arms out towards the lights. *What beautiful lights*, she thought. She rolled the car window down and reached her hand out into the open air. She could almost grab the colors, but every time she closed her hands they would slip through her fingers. She looked back at everyone else wondering if they were feeling the same way. They all seemed to be focused on the road. She could not understand how they could just sit there with a straight face while all these feelings ran wild.

What is this feeling? she thought. She wanted to cry not understanding what she was going through. Lost in a world she did not understand, she fell in love. *I wanna live in it. I wanna die in it,* she thought. With both hands out in the air, she reached out and stuck her head out the car window. The chilling air felt bittersweet. She looked into the sky. She saw nothing, not even the night stars. It was all engulfed by a shroud of clouds, "I hope it rains. Make it rain for me, please," she whispered to the gods. A raindrop crashed down on her forehead.

"More. More. More," Persela whispered to the heavens. The rain began to pick up. She could not help but smile at the idea that even God granted her every wish. Persela tried to climb out of the car. She wanted to feel the rain all over her body. She squeezed her torso out. Reaching her hands into the air, she almost fell out but Anthony managed to pull her back in. She looked at Anthony for a split second and without hesitation kissed him. She looked into his eyes as she pulled away from his lips. Anthony wasn't able to do the same. He looked away pretending to look out the window. He stared at a homeless man on the street curb. Another appeared from a back alley.

Anthony glanced back towards Persela, who was still admiring him. He was beginning to regret having pulled her back into the car. He should have let her fall. He smiled at the idea. She smiled back and stared at him. Anthony could tell she was waiting for some kind of response. He turned to look at Josh, who was busy on his phone. Anthony decided to do the same.

"Let's get something to eat," Helene said. She turned around to look at Anthony and Persela. "Where do y'all prefer?"

"Watch out!" yelled Josh. He pointed at a homeless man who had sprinted into the middle of the street. Helene jerked the steering wheel. She managed to maneuver around the homeless man, but lost control of the car. Helene turned to the right hoping the car would straighten out. Nothing. She turned it to the left. The car ignored every attempt to stabilize and continued to turn uncontrollably. Persela closed her eyes as Helene released the steering wheel.

The car had stopped moving. *I'm dead*, Persela thought. No one moved or said anything. Helene frantically reached into her purse and pulled out a cigarette. She tried to gently place it into her mouth, but her hands would not stop shaking. She pressed it between her lips, but still it managed to slip off.

"Goddamnit! Goddamnit! That was my last fuckin' cigarette."

Persela's heartbeat felt as if it wanted to rip through her ribcage. She looked down at herself. Not a scratch on her. She looked back up and everything began to start spinning. Her stomach felt tight. She needed to release the tension, but it was already climbing up her throat.

"Let me out! Let me out!" Persela shouted. She opened the door and fell on her knees. She tried to stand up but collapsed again. Saliva ran down her lips. She spat it out onto the pavement. She raised her head and noticed a garbage can on the sidewalk.

"Oh. My. Fucking. God," Anthony said. No one responded as the rain continued. Josh looked over at Helene, who was still shaking. Josh looked at Anthony, who seemed to be the only one who found the accident amusing and exhilarating. Josh was ready to say something when without warning he opened his door and vomited.

"I'm ready to go home," Josh said.

"Le-le-let's wait for Per-Per-Persela to finish," Helene faintly insisted.

"You guys hear that?" Anthony said looking around the car.

"Yea," Josh responded. They both knew what they were hearing but did not want to admit it; both hoping that the other would disprove them but none of them said a word. "I hear," he said and then gave Helene a deadly look, "We got to get the fuck out of here!"

Persela's throat burned as she vomited into the trash can. She wished it would stop. She tried convincing herself that she was in a bad dream and, any minute now, she would wake up in her bedroom. When she stopped vomiting, she looked around. Everything was blurry at first, but when her vision cleared, she saw nobody around. Alone and scared, the urge to cry grew within her. She began to shiver in the cold rain. She heard Helene's voice in the distance. She turned and saw Anthony. She raised her hands in the air like an infant expecting to be swept off her feet.

Chapter IV

Leo always found some comfort walking in a city shrouded in darkness. Something about the empty streets seemed hypnotic and distracted him from his problems, but the walk that he had intended to be a short midnight stroll had lasted longer. He had been out nearly all night and was making his way back home when he noticed a car in the middle of the road and a girl standing over a garbage can. Leo watched from a distance.

"Persela!" a girl yelled.

"Fuck!" a male voice cried. It seemed he was getting frustrated at the driver.

"Fuck her. Fuck this shit!" yelled another male. "This is serious jail time compared to Persela's situation. Helene! Come the fuck on! Bitch, I got more drugs than a fucking pharmacy!"

"Helene come on we gotta get the fuck outa here!" the other male yelled. She frantically looked at them and then back at Persela before grabbing the steering wheel with both hands. Leo watched as the car drove off. When the car disappeared, the girl they had abandoned laid on the ground with her hands extended into the air. She tried to get up but failed and finally leaned against the trash can. Police sirens could be heard from a distance.

"Hey!" Leo yelled. He waited for a response. He hastened toward the young girl and heard her snoring. He leaned over to see her face, but her bangs and wild tangled hair hide her identity. Her wet body was trembling uncontrollably. He wanted to get her a cab, but to where? He did not see a purse so discovering her address was impossible. Leo crouched down and a long-lost memory flooded his mind. Without hesitation, he picked her up, tucked her face against his chest, and began to carry her the two blocks to his home.

As he approached his building, two police vehicles passed them. One of the cop cars sharply made a left turn as the other, noticing Leo, slowly made a U-turn. It pulled up next to him. Leo stopped and stood still. He kept a calm posture as he waited for the policeman to exit his vehicle. He never did nor did he bother to turn his headlights off. Leo looked down and away from the bright lights. When the policeman stepped out, he shined his flashlight onto Leo's face. Leo sighed, trying to hold back what he wanted to say.

"Excuse me, sir," he said with a concerned tone. "Have you happened to see a blue car pass by? We got a phone call about a supposed accident."

"Sorry, I have not," Leo said somewhat annoyed as the cop continued to shine his flashlight at his face. The cop looked down at the girl passed out in his arms.

"What about a girl?" he said moving the flashlight away from Leo and towards Persela. "We have a report that a girl was left behind."

Leo wondered who else witnessed the scene. He looked away from the cop and towards the buildings trying to spot sudden movement between window curtains.

"Sorry, officer, I can't help you," Leo snapped. "I must get going now. I do not want my wife to catch a cold."

The officer coughed and took a step back, allowing Leo to pass.

Leo entered his large tower. His footsteps echoed as he walked towards Larry, who was sitting at the concierge stand trying to look busy. Leo looked down at Persela again. She appeared to be dryer than when he found her. He wished he could have said the same about himself.

"I hope you had a marvelous night, Master Leo," Larry declared in his monotone as he got to his feet to bow down. Leo always wondered if he spoke that way even after work. Larry looked over Leo's shoulder and saw a trail of water. A frown came to his face. "I see Clairis had a delightful and enchanting night," he said trying not to seem bothered by the inconvenience.

"Yes, she did," Leo replied with a smile as he re-adjusted his grasp around the unknown girl. He thought about telling Larry that he was not carrying his Clairis but someone else, but who and why?

Larry watched as Leo struggled to maintain his grip. He could not help but ask. "Is there any way I can be of assistance, Master Leo?" Persela's heel slipped off her foot.

"No, I'm fine. Thank you, Larry," Leo replied as he made his way to the elevator.

Larry jumped up to grab the shoe and followed behind. *He is quite mobile for an elderly man*, Leo thought.

"Thank you, Larry," Leo said as he tried to reach over for the fallen heel.

"Please sir, I'll hold on to this and you, Clairis," Larry suggested as they entered the elevator.

On the ride up, Larry shared a story about when he worked for an elevator company. He started to explain that what is seen in Hollywood movies, about elevators falling, was not true. Before Larry could finish, they reached the top floor. The doors slid open to a hallway where a set of double doors with marvelous patterns of bronze and gold stood. Leo walked towards them and carefully pressed his thumb on the wall. The doors opened inward like the entrance to heaven. Leo walked inside and carried Persela through a trail of rose petals that had been intended for Clairis.

"Ummm, you can throw the shoe wherever really," Leo shouted. "I'll pick it up later."

Larry had never been on the top floor. No one had. Making his way inside, he noticed a scripture written in gold on top of the double door. It seemed to be a different language. He peaked inside and saw a luxurious living room but no TV. A bottle of champagne and two crystal champagne flutes rested on top a glass table that was surrounded by black couches. Beyond the living room, dark clouds moved furiously around the building, but not a single drop of water hit the glass windows that surrounded the penthouse. For the first time, Larry wondered how tall the building was. Inside, he stood in the middle and placed the heel on the couch. He looked left and right as if a simple glance both ways would uncover the floors layout. He made his way back hearing Leo returning.

"Thank you, Larry," Leo said as he removed his wet blazer and tossing it on the floor. Walking back towards Larry, he took off his gloves and tossed them on the floor. "It's late, Larry, and I know your day has just started, but mine just ended." Without saying goodnight, Leo shut the door and intently regretted it. He lowered his head in disappointment and sighed. *I should have at least said good night*, he thought. He held onto the door handles as he debated whether to open the door and apologize. He hesitated and then, releasing the handles, deciding it would only make the situation awkward. *I should still apologize, had it not been for him I would have probably had a harder time getting up here.*

Larry made his way back to the elevator. *He must be excruciatingly exhausted,* he thought. Stepping into the elevator he heard his name being called.

"Larry," Leo yelled. He turned around to see Leo's head sticking out the door. He waited to hear Leo's wishes. "Have a wonderful day."

"Of course, Master Leo," Larry replied. Leo smiled. It stretched from ear-to-ear and exposed all his pearly white teeth. Larry

42

could not help but smile back. "The same goes towards you, Master Leo."

Leo sighed as he walked to the middle of the room, where he stood staring at the roiling clouds. *There is a stranger sleeping in my home,* he thought. Leo rubbed his forehead and then sat on the couch. His hands fidgeted. He looked up at the ceiling and then around the villa. Nothing grabbed his attention until his eyes landed on the bottle of champagne. Leo grabbed it. *Why Leo?* he asked himself. He felt weak minded for a moment and then placed it back on the table. Instead, he grabbed a crystal flute and walked into the kitchen where he filled it with water from the faucet.

"I'll stay awake until she wakes up and explain the situation. Hopefully, she'll understand." He took a sip. "She could have died out there! What was I supposed to do? Let her die?" He frowned then looked down at the dripping faucet. "I did the right thing."

He turned on his phone on and looked at all his notifications. They were all from Clairis, fifty-six missed calls, twenty-one voicemails, and one hundred and three text messages. So many calls, voicemails, and texts made him question how she really felt about him. He thought about her and their time together. He wondered whether he should listen to at least one of her voicemails or read one text. Maybe one out of the twenty-one voicemails or one out of the hundred and three text messages contained a good explanation. He was about to check when he realized nothing she could say could help her cause. Clairis had slept with another man. He thought back to that night wondering why he had acted the way he did.

"Oh, I'm so sorry. Please excuse me. Where are my manners? I should have knocked first," Leo remembered explaining when he walked in on her affair. He kept control and turned away. *I should have killed him right there.* He heard the bed sheets move frantically as Clairis ran after him. He ignored her pleas. *I should have turned around. Why didn't I?*

Leo took another sip of water. *Why?* he thought as he made his way to the window. His reflection appeared in the glass. Studying the man that stood before him, he could not help but feel disappointed. Lightning struck, but the flash of light was soon engulfed by darkness. Leo watched as another lightning bolt lit up the sky. The clouds swirled. With his free hand, Leo reached over and placed his fingertips on the window. Another lightning bolt struck closer to the building. The vibration tickled his fingertips as it shook the building. Leo felt privileged to be able to stand next to God as he struck his divine and powerful instrument amongst the world. He sipped water from his champagne glass as lightning struck in every direction and gracefully danced through the sky. The city below looked broken and on the verge of shattering.

What a beautiful mess, he thought as the thunder arrived and the floor beneath his feet trembled. Leo looked down at the city and hoped he would see someone who would distract him from the chaos but the thick clouds made it impossible. He was surrounded by darkness. Trapped in a world that felt far away from any living thing, he felt a sharp pain in his chest. The pain grew as the lightning ceased. Everything became dark again. His reflection reappeared.

"Have I really reached such magnitude and yet," he paused, "and yet, still be destitute?" Leo looked down at the world and although he stood next to a divine force, he felt as if someone more important was missing.

Inside Leo's bedroom, Persela tossed and turned as she dreamt being elsewhere. She was standing at the edge of a curb with no umbrella as rain savagely poured down on her. Across the street, a building harbored women with beautiful dresses and gorgeous men in suits. They were all dancing to an old rhythm and beat. Persela had never seen anyone dance the way they did. Others sat around small round tables laughing hysterically with one another. All the men were smoking large cigars as the women smoked cigarettes. The scene made them look old fashioned, something out of the 40's or older. It did not matter to her. She wanted to join them. Her body ached to move. She was ready to dance her way over when a man took notice of Persela standing outside. He puffed on his cigar. He smiled, exposing his cunning good looks. Embarrassed, Persela stood still not understanding why she felt ashamed. The man walked away from his group of friends and disappeared. The door opened and he made his way over to her. She felt a surge of warmth surrounding her. She wanted to walk away, but her body would not move. For the first time in her life, she was intimidated by a man. He stopped and stretched his hand out towards her. The simple gesture overwhelmed her as it was something unfamiliar to her. Not knowing what else to do, her hand extended towards his. He smiled. Her heart stood still as his face was as sharp and smooth as a cunning blade. She recognized him from somewhere. She could not quite connect his face with a name, but she had met this man before. Grabbing hold of her hand, he led her towards the party.

The music was louder than she thought. She glanced around noticing people laughing and dancing. When they sat down on a small wooden table, she noticed she was wearing a cloche hat and a red and black beaded drop-waist dress. She looked around in awe. On stage, a band played music using instruments that seemed to have been constructed out of kitchen appliances and dumpster parts. Nonetheless, the music was not like anything she had ever heard of. It made her feel alive and want to move. She looked at the mysterious man. Puffing on his cigar, he blew the smoke at her face. She blinked and before the smoke cleared, she was out on the dance floor with him. Her dress twirled as he spun her around. She danced as if she knew every step. She moved like she had always known how to. She wore a smile that was more attracting than her dress. Filled with excitement, she wanted to know his name. His lips moved, but she could not hear him clearly as the music grew louder and louder. She stopped dancing in frustration. She pressed her hands up against her ears attempting to block the noise, but nothing changed. She pressed harder and closed her eyes, but the noise only seemed to get louder.

Waking up from the dream, Persela looked around in confusion. Then, without warning, she felt something crawling up her throat. Her insides burned as if she had been eaten hot coal the night before. She examined the enormous bed surrounded with rose petals and vomit. Disgusted, she crawled to the edge of the bed. She looked around trying to remember where she was, but nothing came to mind. She tried to focus as the loud music slowly faded into smooth jazz. She looked for something that might help her regain her memory. Nothing jogged her mind. She searched inside her bra for her phone. It was gone. Her hands frantically searched the bed. She jumped up and pulled all the covers off. Nothing. She put her head underneath the bed, and reached her arm as far as she could. Still nothing.

"Shit!" she told herself. Trying to calm her mind, she tried thinking of the last thing she had done the night before. Thinking back, she remembered being at a bar with three men who wanted to sleep with her. *Oh, hell no*, Persela thought. The thought of sleeping with any of those disgusting men sobered her a little. Her mind was now intoxicated with fear and disappointment. She had committed something she was going to regret for the rest of her life. *How could this have happened?* she thought. Finding her heels next to the bed, she quickly put them on. Using her hand as a comb, she straightened her tangled hair as she prepared herself for what stood on the other side of the bedroom door.

She creaked open the door and looked around. She saw no one, just an enormous living room with nice furniture. She could smell freshly cooked breakfast, though. The smell of toasted bread and eggs entered her nostrils and crept down to her stomach. Her stomach growled angrily. She looked around and noticed her phone on the floor next to the furniture. Then she saw an enormous bronze door.

Must be the exit, she thought as she stared at it. She stood frozen attempting to think of a plan to leave unseen. She was scared of stepping out and discovering her worst fears had happened. "Maybe Anthony brought me here. Maybe everyone pitched in and got this room, and I don't remember. It's probably Helene cooking right now, and I'm just overreacting," Persela said to herself in an attempt to ease her mind. The idea somewhat comforted her. "That makes sense. These kinds of things happen." She glanced around the living room again and noticed a breathtaking sunrise. She felt queasy seeing the sun at that height. She could only imagine what floor they were on. "I think these kinds of things happen." Before doubting her comforting idea, she walked out.

Leo had awakened on the sofa and having forgotten about Clairis' affair and about picking up a young girl off the city streets. He had resumed his routine of playing some of his favorite tracks as he cooked breakfast. Reaching under the granite table, he grabbed a plate. As he placed it on the table, he discovered someone else standing inside his villa. A young girl stared at him with surprise. Leo also fell into a state of confusion. For a split second, he had no idea who she was or where she had come from. As Leo's memories returned, he realized something else.

"Hey," Leo said recognizing the young girl, "Persela, right?"

Persela stood motionless not knowing what to think. No matter how hard she thought back, she could not figure out how she ended up with him. *I fucking slept with the asshole who wouldn't buy me a shot!* was all that she could think.

"You hungry?" Leo asked still grinning. He pulled out a stool from under the granite table. He reached back and pulled out another plate.

Persela stood for a moment. *Had she really slept with him? He seems just as surprised as I am,* she thought. She glanced at the stool he had pulled out and the breakfast he had prepared. Her stomach growled loud enough that Leo heard. He turned around to face her and smiled the same way he did when she had met him at the bar. There was something about his smile she liked so much. She approached the stool. Leo walked around her when she sat. He approached the couch and grabbed the full bottle of champagne. Persela looked down at the freshly cooked eggs and toasted bread. Her mouth began to water. Her stomach growled furiously again. Yet, she did not accept his kindness. She glanced at Leo, who was picking up his blazer jacket and making his way to the opposite side of the villa. She could have left that very moment while he was not looking, but before the idea could cross her mind, he returned.

"It's going to get cold," Leo suggested. He grabbed Persela's phone from the floor and placed it on the kitchen table. She grabbed it and returned it to her bra. She looked down at the food awkwardly while Leo stood at the counter waiting for her to take a bite.

"Do you have a fork?" she asked. She could not help but feel uneasy in front of him. She thought about resting her elbows on the table but didn't. She could almost hear him, *no elbows on the table*. She awkwardly placed her hands on her lap.

"Oh, I am so sorry," Leo placed a fork and spoon next to her meal. Leo still waited for her to take a bite. Since nobody had ever tasted his cooking, he was curious to know what she thought, but Persela did not know that. She just felt the weight of his presence.

"Crap," Leo whispered under his breath. He walked over a metallic wall near the stove and slid a cabinet door open. It was a refrigerator.

"Wow," she said under her breath. He reached in and took out a gallon of orange juice. Holding it with one hand, he reached over the refrigerator and pushed in another metallic wall. It slid open. He took out two glass cups and sat across from Persela.

"So about last night," Leo started. He slowly poured orange juice into the first glass. Persela stopped breathing. "What do you remember?"

"Nothing," Persela whispered and dropped her eyes to look at her meal. Leo replied with a blank face, clearly unhappy about her answer. He started pouring the second cup.

"Your friends," Leo started as he slid her a glass of orange juice. He stopped and tapped his fingers on the table as he pondered what to say. Persela could not help but look down at his hands. They looked distorted and hideous. His knuckles seemed monstrous as veins stretched from his wrist to the tip of his fingers. But what bothered her the most was the scar that stretched across his hands right above his knuckles. She froze and gasped in fear. He was a dangerous man, and although she had no proof, his hands were of no angel.

Chapter V

Rachel pleaded, "Please slow down," as they squeezing through a crowd of pedestrians. Clairis ignored her and continued pushing through a crowd of men, who glared at Clairis with a nasty look. "What makes you so sure he's even there?"

"Because Robert told me!"

"What'd he tell you?"

"That he owns that building and someone in there is bound to know where he is!" Clairis explained as she forced another man out of her path.

"Damn, bitch," he said under his breath. Clairis was not bothered. She was focused on what she was doing. Nothing was going to distract her. She squeezed her way to the front of a crowd of people waiting at the crosswalk. As she waited to make it to the other side, she tapped her foot lightly on the pavement. Clairis looked at the street lights, which were still red. Nothing seemed to change. She looked both ways. She was going to cross.

"Clairis, no! No! No! No! No! No!" Rachel screeched as Clairis walked into oncoming traffic. Rachel tried to apologize to everyone as she hurled herself forward with Clairis. A driver honked his horn at them.

"I'm so sorry," Rachel yelled. When Rachel reached the other side, she jolted onward nibbling on her lower lip in frustration.

How strange, Rachel thought. *Clairis is not the kind of woman to fall for a man.* "So, what's so special about this guy anyways?" Rachel finally asked. "Is it the money?"

Clairis stopped and spun around to face Rachel. Her curly red hair whipped around and landed on her face. "How kewd jew evehn say dat?" Rachel already regretting what she had said. Clairis was losing control of her French accent and did not bother to readjust herself. She just continued glaring at Rachel.

"I mean... I'm sorry. It's just that you've never really gave me the inside scoop on you two," Rachel explained in her defense. "You've never even introduced me to him. I don't even know what he looks like." The fire in Clairis' eyes cooled down. Relieved, Rachel rubbed her arm awkwardly. Clairis had not introduced Leo to Rachel or anyone else. She only said she was seeing a man and that was as far as the conversation ever went. It's not that she wanted to keep him a secret, but it seemed Leo wanted to keep himself away from Clairis and everyone she was aquatinted with. Rachel knew as much about Leo as Clairis did. What more could she tell her closest friend besides that she was seeing a man named Leo?

"I'm sorry," Clairis sighed and continued walking.

"So, how did you two meet?" Rachel asked. She saw a smile appear on Clairis' face.

"I met him at a fundraiser for Robert's campaign race. It was actually Robert who introduced me to him. Rob explained Leo as, 'my kind of guy.' I wondered what he meant by that and had to meet what my kind of guy was. He was sitting at the bar alone looking off into space," Clairis looked up at the sky for a moment. "He introduced me to him. Leo didn't seem too much interested in me so nothing happened that night."

"Ok," Rachel said waiting for Clairis to continue but it seemed she was reminiscing.

"Leo," Clairis said smiling. "I saw him in St. Petersburg, Russia. Me and Oksana went to the Bachata Festival."

"Where was I?" Rachel asked annoyed.

"Doing that photo shoot in Paris," Clairis snapped and Rachel frowned. "Anyways," she continued, "I was at the festival where everyone was being taught the steps by the dance instructor. He was just standing alone in the back. I went up and asked if he needed a dance partner. I recognized him, but I don't think he recognized me. We danced. He danced well," Clairis said.

Rachel wondered what she was referring to.

"He danced so well I thought he was Latin American or something. I thought he was. I think he is. But I don't know. Anyways, we spent the entire event together and from then he asked me if I wanted to fly to Turkey with him."

"So, that's it?" Rachel asked expecting more to her story. "What was he doing in St. Petersburg? Was he stalking you," she joked.

"No," Clairis said laughing exposing the dimples in her cheeks. "He said he was there for a business trip."

"So, what does he do?" Rachel asked seeing this as an opportunity to get some information about Leo.

"Honestly. I don't really know," Clairis looked down in disappointment. "See, this is what I hated about Leo. The only reason I know he owns the skyscraper is because Robert just told me yesterday. He never let me in his life. Je ne sais rien de lui! Quel genre de relations eil que!"

Clairis started ranting in French. Rachel tried her best to just listen.

"What kind of relationship is that? A relationship where you don't even know what your boyfriend does for a living? I don't know anything about you! I've never met your parents," Claris ranted as though Leo were in front of her. Everything she had held in for so long was now coming out. "Why do you travel across every continent? And those God damn gloves!"

Gloves, Rachel thought. "Ok, ok," pleaded Rachel. "It's gonna be ok, Clairis."

The rest of the walk was silent. Rachel kept her distance from Clairis as she tried to put everything together. Rachel had always understood Clairis, or so it had seemed. She had known her for years now. Rachel had been a model for some time when Clairis had barely started. They could relate with one another having gone through the same childhood and grown into the same business. It was only natural that they quickly latched on to each other and became friends. Clairis was a nature-loving free-spirited soul whose optimism was contagious. She loved interacting with people and energized those around her. Her beauty had to also be credited. She was a fine piece of creation. Her body was slim, but displayed the attributes of womanhood. Her wavy brown hair hung elegantly down to her mid-back and although she recently colored it red her beauty was unaffected. Her ivy green eyes would cast her admirers into a hedge maze. Her lips were even more interesting. The edges held an upward arc that gave the appearance that she was always smiling. Now, as Rachel watched her friend walk furiously through the city, Clairis appeared like a mad woman with blazing red hair, piercing eyes with the ability to project poison, and a natural smile that was more cynical than pleasing. It seemed she no longer knew Clairis, and it was all caused by a single man.

Rachel found it strange because Clairis viewed men the same way she did fashion, always moving on the next trendy style. And even when she met a man she genuinely liked, she would always recite her stock phrase before breaking up, "I'm a free-spirited soul that no one can imprison." It appeared that commitment was never something she was looking for. Yet here she was as if she had cared for this man, grown attached, perhaps even fallen in love.

When they reached the skyscraper, they walked inside. A convention of some sort was going on. Men and women in professional attire walked about conversing with one another. Rachel and Clairis wearing simple jeans and regular tank tops seemed out of place. Clairis did not mind as a group of people glanced her way. Unlike

Clairis, Rachel was somewhat embarrassed. She smiled and deeply apologized as she walked through the busy men and women.

On the top floor, the doors opened to a hallway with an intimidating double door. Clairis had appeared confident the entire walk, but now that she was there she seemed to regret coming at all. She stood there petrified for a minute. Then, a young girl in a tight dress came speed walking towards them.

Rachel gently pushed Clairis out of the elevator so that the young girl could get through. Clairis had never seen her before. She seemed to not have noticed them, but Clairis kept a close eye on her as she entered the elevator. When the elevator doors shut, Clairis broke from her trance and bolted towards the double doors before they closed. Leo was reaching down to grab his gloves when Clairis barged in. Leo turned his back on her, suggested her to leave him be.

"She's pretty," Clairis said. Leo said nothing. "So, who was that?" Clairis demanded as she walked towards Leo. "Answer me!" Her heroic character began to deteriorate as her bottom lip trembled. "Répondez-moi!" Tears began to flow down her cheeks.

"Elle n'était personne importante," Leo answered. His perfect French caused Rachel to assume that he was French but then Leo greeted Rachel in perfect Russian, "And you must be Rachel. It is a pleasure to finally make your acquaintance. I am-"

Stomping her foot like a child Clairis yelled, "Who was she, Leo?" She wiped tears from her cheek with the back of her hands and tried to not lose control of her emotions. No women, not even Clairis, had ever been to his villa. Clairis could not help but feel offended at witnessing a random woman walk out. "Who was she," she demanded again. Clairis looked over Leo's shoulder where she noticed all the rose petals scattered over his penthouse. Her heart stopped and broke into pieces.

"Clairis, she was no one. Please. I do not question who you spend your days and nights with. Do not question who I spend mine with." His words cut deep inside her. He was right. He never did question what she did during her nights out. He had not even asked who the man was who she had been sleeping with.

"Why didn't you question me? Why weren't you overprotective? Did you never have the slightest bit of feeling for me?" she yelled. "Huh. Why?" For the first time, she felt unwanted, and it agitated her. "I'm sorry, Leo," she pleaded in a now soft voice. "Please, forgive me."

"You feel remorseful, Clairis," he declared. He reached his hand over to hold hers. "Please. Like you said, you are 'a free-spirited soul with no one to impose on you with commitment.' I do not plan on imprisoning a divine soul as yours."

Clairis used to love listening him talk. The way he spoke and the words he used were like nothing she'd ever heard from anyone before. He was a poet at heart, and that's why she secretly loved him. Now, Leo wounded her with the words she had once spoken so proudly and with honest conviction. She did feel guilty, guilty that she had betrayed a man who had given her nearly everything she had ever dreamed of. She remembered what Robert had said. He was the kind of guy for her. Sadly, she was not the woman for him.

As Leo released Clairis hand from his grasp, he leaned over to whisper in her ear. Rachel wondered what he was saying to her. Clairis turned around and began walking towards the elevator.

"What did he tell you?" Rachel asked not expecting an answer. Just as she predicted, she got none.

Chapter VI

"You think she's fucken dead?" Anthony was pacing around Josh's dorm when he reached into his notebook. He ripped a section from a piece of paper and created little paper ball. He tossed it into a trash bin that stood in the far back corner. "You think you could live with that. I mean if she died you know."

"Bro, she took some fuckin' sass. Clean sass. Not laced shit. It wasn't heroin. Sass. Relax," Josh said typing on his laptop. "Besides, if she did die. It's not so bad when you're on ecstasy."

"So, has Helene texted back?"

"She hasn't texted. Please, smoke something, man. God damn. I got this review due, and I can't do it with you riding my ass. If anything, she's probably locked up, but that's not our problem."

"Yea," was all he said. Anthony jumped on Josh's bed and grabbed a textbook. He opened it and tried to distract himself. An image of Persela popped into his head. He wanted to get rid of it. He felt guilty, and it bothered him. *Why should I? I did nothing wrong. If anything, it was her fault. She should not have taken the sass or gone out with us in the first place.* He dropped the book and picked up another. He was looking through the pages when his phone rang.

Tatyana: *Hey wyd tonight? am i gonna see you?*

Anthony hesitated. He contemplated on what he was going to respond. With no good response, he ignored her text. His phone rang again.

Tatyana: *Helloooooo i'm talking to you*

Anthony looked up as Josh's phone rang. "Who's it from?"

"It's Helene," Josh answered.

"What's it say?"

"Anthony, it just rang. Can I read it, please?" Josh said before reading her text. "So, Persela is home safe and, lucky for you, doesn't remember anything."

"Damn," Anthony said with a smirk on his face. "I can't believe we actually left that bitch." He picked up his phone and quickly replied to Tatyana's text.

Anthony: *Yea I'm come see you tonight.*

"Man, do we like to party, huh?" Josh said as he yawned. Stretching his arms into the air, he got up. "Anyways come on. We're late. As always."

"So, what you do after we got back?"

"Tatyana," Anthony responded. "Oh, my God, man. She's so fuckin' fine, Josh."

"Really? So is Persela. I don't understand what's wrong with Persela."

"Nothing, it's just that Tatyana lets you do whatever you want with her, man."

"Damn, it's like that? You're crazy, you gonna get caught one day."

"Nah, I'm not. But yea with Persela, you gotta be all gentle and shit. It's cool, but sometimes yo boy needs a bit more. So, what's up with you and Helene?"

"It's cool. Tryna make it work," Josh responded.

"Sounds like a lotta work," Anthony said with an agitated smirk. "Sounds like a lot of work. And fuckin' boring honestly."

"Bro, it's a lot of fuckin' work. Helene is a lot of work!"

"Whatchu mean?"

"You know how she is. The whole, 'I grew up with divorced parents so give me all the attention or I'll go smoke weed, party, and whatever to block away the pain.' Which I know is bullshit. Just excuses."

"I don't know why you're with her." Anthony just looked at Josh blankly. Having never been in a situation like Josh's, he did not know how to respond. "Oh, shit, come on. Let's go the other way. Persela like to take this way and I don't feel like dealing with her right now." Anthony suggested.

Chapter VII

Persela walked into her first class, "Morals and Ethics." She sat down and waited for class to begin. It was not long before the empty chairs were filled with students. A husky elderly man with a bald head and snow white beard walked in holding a briefcase and some books. Walking to his desk, he placed his briefcase and a book on the table and then turned to the white board.

"My name is Dr. Schmidt or Dr. S., whichever is easier for you," he said in a soft, gentle tone. "Professor S. is also acceptable." When he stepped aside, Persela saw, "Why?" written on the board. Dr. S. said nothing about what he wrote nor did he suggest what the assignment was. Instead, he sat down on his desk and began reading the book he had brought with him. Students glanced at each other with confusion. Someone quickly pulled out a pencil and paper. Persela, not knowing what to do, just sat in her chair and waited for Dr. S. to explain what the task was. *Why?* Nothing came to mind when she thought about the word. She tried saying it under her breath. Still nothing. And although it made no sense to her, the question made perfect sense to others. The questioned fired a trigger inside those that understood it and rushed to grab their paper and pencil. *Why what?* she thought looking back at the question. Frustrated and confused, she began tapping her pencil on the table.

An hour passed, Dr. S. was still reading. More than half of his students had left. Not understanding the assignment, they saw the class as a waste of time. Persela stayed. She was curious. She looked at the white board and repeated the question over and over. It was a pointless and unnecessary question yet heavy and meaningful. She was stuck in a place where she thought she knew the answer but then wondered if this was even a question that needed answering. Grabbing her pencil, she pressed it against a piece of paper. She was ready to write when the professor's chair squeaked. He dropped his book and turned his attention back to the white board.

"Why not?" he roared. A student jolted to attention and lifted his head to see what the commotion was about. Dr. S. waited for him to regain composure before continuing. As old as he was, his voice was still young and energetic. "Why not?" he started again as if the words were the very core of his existence. He stepped to the side allowing everyone to see the words 'why not,' which were now written underneath what he had already written. Seconds passed.

"Why? Why not? Happiness, wealth, money, love, beauty. All that sounds pleasant." He stopped allowing the words to fly around the classroom and into his students' mind. "Why not filth? Why not poverty? Why not unimportance, loneliness, the ugly?" He paused. "Why not pain? Why not hate?" Stopping once more, he glanced around the room. Looking at his students, he finished by saying, "And why not self-honesty?"

No one spoke. Their eyes were glued to Dr. S. as they waited for him to continue. Persela leaned on the edge of her seat. Her mind was racing with ideas. She was ready to respond.

"I think we should always be happy," Persela argued. Dr. S. looked at Persela with a blank face waiting for her to explain. "The truth is we're all meant to be happy. No one deserves any less."

"What if someone's purpose, someone's truth. Maybe even their destiny was to be miserable and unhappy?"

"What would be the purpose of living that kind of life?" Persela snapped. "What kind of life would that be? Who would ever want to live like that?"

Dr. S. chuckled. "As long as someone is happy. Someone out there is miserable," he whispered as the bell rang.

Persela walked out of the classroom without hearing his response.

"Helene!" Persela yelled with excitement.

"Baby," Helene said, "why didn't you text me that you got to class safe? What is more important than texting me that you're safe?" Helene played with her nails as she waited for an explanation.

"I love you, Helene," Persela said pouting. Helene's disgusted face disappeared. Persela noticed a slight redness under Helene's nose.

"Coffee just doesn't do it anymore, Honey," Helene moaned to herself. "You want some of the Molly you had that night or whatever that was?"

Looking past Helene, Persela noticed Anthony walking down the hallway with Josh. "Who's Molly?" she asked.

"I said to have some, not all," Josh said snatching the bag away from Helene. His aggravation did not stop him from leaning over to kiss her.

"Come on, Babe," Helene protested.

"Anyways I got to go," Josh said looking down the hallway. "I'll see you tonight."

"I'll walk with you," Helene said desperately. She looked back at Persela and smiled brightly like a shooting star. Josh walked away with Helene and they disappeared into a crowd of students. Persela turned to face Anthony. Anthony could read exactly what her face was saying, but he was already annoyed with her. He knew she was expecting him to walk her to her next class. He did not want to, but he felt the need to show Persela off and remind everyone that she belonged to him.

"Umm, do you want me to walk you to class?" Anthony asked. Persela nodded and smiled. Reaching over, she tightly wrapped her arms around his. Anthony lightly grated his teeth in frustration.

"You make me so happy," Persela said rubbing her head against his shoulder.

"Alright," was all Anthony said as they arrived at her class. He jerked his arm back and left without saying another world.

Persela entered her new class and showed interest in it just like she did with every other. Because of that, she was quickly noticed and admired by her professors and the other students. She was not afraid to ask a question and constantly gave her opinion on a subject. At times, it seemed she was interrupting, but the professor gladly allowed her to speak. No one seemed offended. People couldn't help but grow curious about Persela intelligence. After every class, everyone approached her, hoping to gain a new friend.

As she walked out of her last class, Persela was surrounded by people vying for her attention. She loved being showered with affection and tried to give everyone the attention they deserved. As they walked through the hallways, everyone wondered if she was some sort of star and could not help but approach her entourage.

"Hey, Babe," Anthony said shoving the crowd of students. He leaned in and kissed her passionately. "She's taken," he told the crows of students. "That means you too ladies."

Anthony wrapped his arms around Persela protectively. She giggled and blushed for a second. The awkward silence that followed finally chased the crowd away. Walking out the building hand-in-hand, they made their way down the courtyard where Anthony heard someone rushing up from behind him. Over his shoulder, Anthony saw a brown-skinned male with long uncombed hair, and an incorrectly buttoned flannel making his way towards them. *Another student late for class*, Anthony thought.

"So how was your day, babe?" he asked trying to sound interested.

"Persela!" yelled the student. Persela released Anthony and turned around.

"Hey, I know this might not be the right time, but I was wondering if I could get your number," he said. He pulled his phone out and handed it to Persela. "I really liked what you said in Dr. S class. I wanna hear more."

"What?" Anthony said as his upper lip twitched.

"Yea?" her eyes widened. "I had no idea someone was actually listening to me," she said. She felt honored that someone wanted to hear more of her opinions.

"Hey, fuck off, man," Anthony intervened, but it was too late. He was already putting his phone back in his pocket. The browned skinned male simply glanced at Anthony, who grated his teeth not knowing how to respond. He looked back to where Josh typically would be. Anthony's face turned light red with anger. He felt weak and hopeless without Josh.

"Thanks, and I'll see you later in Dr. S's class," he said and before leaving in a rush he looked back at Persela, "oh and my name is Marc, by the way." Anthony thought about grabbing him by his shirt and dragging him off campus.

"I'll meet you back at your dorm. Josh said he wanted to speak to me. I'll be back later," Anthony said walking away from her. He thought about smashing Persela's phone into the concrete but could not bring himself to do it. *Fuck her*, he thought.

"Ok, well, I'll see you later, right?" Persela said as she watched Anthony walk away.

"I'll see."

"My profile always shows my location so you'll always find me," Persela yelled.

"Profile?" Anthony wondered and then realized she was talking about a social networking site where, if he ever needed to, he could pinpoint her location. He wondered when he would ever need to use that feature. *Fuckin' never*, he thought laughing.

Chapter VIII

Anthony walked towards a bar where he was meeting Josh. He wondered why he wanted to talk in private. It slightly bothered him. Why not somewhere else more comfortable like Josh's dorm or even his own dorm? What could be so classified that they needed to meet in the city and away from campus? Walking down a street, a cold and bitter gust of wind blew through him. Winter was on its way. Anthony saw Josh inside the bar. He was sitting next to the window already drinking.

"So, what's all this about?" asked Anthony. Josh sipped some of his beer and then decided to jump straight to the point.

"Why do you want to join The Pool Table Club?" Josh asked. Anthony was taken by surprise. He raised his hand and rubbed his forehead as he thought of an answer. Josh waited.

"Oh, so this is what this is about."

"Yea. What the fuck did you think this was about? So why? I mean when I kinda told you who they were and that they were interested in you. I didn't think you would actually accept the offer. So why do you wanna join?" Josh asked again.

"Well," Anthony stopped to think about his response. "I want something different. I'm tired of the same thing every day. Like. Like," he grew frustrated at not being able to express his thoughts. "Like Persela, girls in general." An image of Persela came into Anthony's mind as well of all the other girls he had been with. He had enjoyed manipulating women but now he wanted something more. He wanted power over more than just a woman. "I want to amount to something great," he said with conviction.

"So why The Pool Table Club?" Josh repeated.

"It's gonna sound weird but I feel like that's where I'm supposed to be. Like its calling out to me." Anthony was beginning to recall more of his reasons. "I want to make something of myself. I want to build an empire. And I feel like The Pool Table Club is gonna help me do it. Besides, I'm tired of being under my father's shadow."

"So, I talked to Ben the other day," Josh declared. Anthony lit up with excitement.

"What did he say?"

"They're going to call you in some time. I don't know exactly when. But the reason I wanted to talk to you is... I wanted to talk to you about the society." Josh paused as he tried to put words together. "I was spotted by a brother freshman year and, for some fuckin' reason, he asked if I wanted to join. I had never heard of the club before so I think he was pulling my leg because no one had ever heard of The Pool Table Club. As far as anyone was concerned, it doesn't exist. When he gave me the tour inside the house I nearly had a heart attack. I knew I had to join. I figured it would be the right thing to do since it would help me after college." Josh stopped speaking again, looked over his shoulder, and then began to whisper. "After a year in the club, I find out that it is more than what I thought. I mean, it's hard to describe it. Like for example, there is literally nothing The Pool Table Club cannot get and cannot do. I don't want to say much, but the initiation or hazing or whatever you want to call it, it's not what you expect."

"Anything?" Anthony said and the word echoed in his head.

Josh tried again, "Like I heard politicians, government officials, and other people are involved."

"Oh, you heard?" Anthony remarked. "I mean it's a frat. What politician isn't in one?"

"I know! It's just different. God damn, just listen!" Josh roared. He was getting frustrated with himself not being able to dissuade Anthony from joining. "It's weird. It's like everything they do has a purpose. Everything is a plan." He paused to look away then back. "Well, when they do call you in, and you join. Just," he paused and then said, "just stay on your feet 'cause they want you in their club for a reason and I'm not gonna fuckin' be there all the time."

The discussion ended, and the mood quickly changed. Anthony ordered a beer and they talked and laughed a bit.

"So, what was up with you and Persela that one night?"

"Man, does she know how to piss me the fuck off. So, I asked her if she wanted to eat and she said 'no' right. Fuck it! She's a grown adult I'm not gonna ask her twice. So, I get a mushroom and Swiss burger."

"Yea. Classic you."

"Anyways, so I order. Step outside to smoke a cigarette. Came back and the bitch is eating my food."

"God damn, only Persela would do some shit like that," Josh said looking at his phone.

"That's not the worst part. The fuckin' bitch picked out all the mushrooms. I swear I was ready to go ballistic," they both laughed as Josh looked at his phone again.

"Damn, I'm late. Next time just order two."

"Helene?" Anthony asked wiping tears of laughter off his face. Josh nodded.

"Oh man, funny shit," Josh said getting up from his seat. They both walked out the bar and without saying another word headed in opposite directions.

The sun was setting as Anthony walked down a crowded city street. He looked down at his phone then up at the tallest skyscraper. He imagined being on the top floor, looking down at busy pedestrians walking about like simple unimportant ants in an ant farm. He laughed at a childhood memory. He was in his back yard holding a magnifying glass, burning ant hills for fun. He stopped laughing when he realized something. He was the unimportant ant. Anthony looked away. He felt weak and controlled by the man who stood on the top floor. That man could have been looking down at him at that very moment. Anthony imagined him being powerful and in control of people's fates, including his very own. He hated that. Anthony wanted to have that power. He wanted to be in control. He wanted to decide others' fates. He wanted to be the kid with the magnifying glass burning all the pitiful ants. He glared up at the tower trying to show whoever was looking down at him that he was not scared. *I'm going to take your place one day*, he thought. A gush of wind blew ferociously. His cheeks turned pink as the cold wind touched his face. Anthony's train of thoughts came to a halt. He crossed an empty street making his way to Tatyana's.

Chapter IX

"Honestly, I'm tired of this. It's just that he could be doing this himself. He could easily just make a fake name on any social network and find out what he wants to know. What do you think, William?" Philip asked. William sighed. "It just bothers me because after all the investigating and information gathering. In the end, all he asks is 'are they well?'"

"You're getting paid so I don't know why this is bothering you," was William's response.

"Yea, I guess I just miss the action. I'm tired of babysitting these people."

"Well, speaking of action. Nothing, he's clean. I kind of figured. I've already arranged everything. Plans have been set in motion."

"Hmmmm, sounds good," Philip stopped. A jogger was approaching them. She disappeared down the track. "Let's talk some other time and somewhere more private."

"How more private can we get? We're in the middle of a jogging trail. Anyways that's really all I got."

"Okay, I've got to go give him the same answer." Philip got up and left Williams, who stayed back to smoke a cigarette and admire a female jogger in shorts.

Philip arrived at a small house where he found Leo sitting in front of a piano. His hands were hovering over the keys as if he was about to start playing. When he heard Philip arrive, Leo turned around and got up.

"Are they well?" Leo asked.

"They are all well and, Leo, I want to talk to you about something."

"Good!" Leo said relieved. He sat down in front of the piano again.

"You know you can do this without me. You can spy on this family." Leo did not respond.

"What about Governor Robert?"

"Clean," Philip snapped. "He's actually clean. He's a cocky prick, but he is clean."

"Well," Leo said. He was mildly aggravated.

"A plan is already underway," Philip answered.

"Philip, we all have a job. I know things aren't as exciting as they once were, but I need you to do your part and continue, please." Leo said getting up and walking towards Phillip.

"Can you play?" Philip asked looking at the piano. He was disappointed by Leo's request so he decided to talk about something else.

"No," Leo said.

Chapter X

April 20, 2011
Even while I'm awake, I dream

Upset, I pushed the drywall gun hard into the wall. I reached into my tool belt to reload.

***

"Join the army with me, brother." Grant suggested. "This my last semester. After this, I'm leaving to basic training."

"College," I replied confidently.

"We can go together. Come on, brother." He could tell I was thinking about it. He knew me so well. "I thought we were brothers?" Grant suggested. He was trying everything to convince me, but I had already made up my mind. Still, the idea of traveling the world and meeting all sorts of people sounded amazing. "What yah scared of?" Grant had asked.

"Getting shot!" I replied. When I looked his way, Grant was laughing.

"Punk. I thought you weren't afraid of gettin' shot?"

"Because I didn't have a choice at the time. Here I am with the opportunity to go to school and go to college and guess what? I don't have to worry about getting shot!" I laughed.

"What yah wanna to go to college for anyways?"

"I'm thinking teacher." I entered an empty classroom filled with computers and Grant leaned on the wall by the door.

"Think about it. I'm off. Me, Oreo, and Hope are ditching school," Grant said as he walked away. I looked back confused.

"Hope ditching school?" I thought. I wanted to say something like, "Hope should not be skipping school," or "don't drag Hope into your lifestyle," but it was too late. Grant had already disappeared.

***

"Fierro!" yelled someone behind me. I didn't turn to see who it was. It only made me work faster.

"Otra!" I yelled putting the last screw on. Before I could think or consider resting, Carlos was already behind me with another sheetrock. He smacked it up against the wall and slid it towards the one I had just put up.

"Aye, una luce," Carlos yelled. I bent over. Hanging my drill gun on my tool belt, Carlos handed me the router. Drilling the outlet out, I was suffocated by white powder.

***

"So, with this program, you can create a resume and send them to any college you want to apply for."

I looked on the screen scanning all the questions. They were basic questions about me nothing I couldn't figure out. My fingertips twitched. I wanted to fill everything in and be the first one to finish. I scanned every question, already answering them inside my head. Then I came across a question I could not answer. "What is your social security number?"

***

74

I continued to aggressively push the screws into the wall. A drop of sweat crawled down my forehead and toward my eyelid. I tried blinking it away, but it made no difference.

***

"What do you mean you don't have a social security number?" the woman asked. She looked over my shoulder and onto the computer screen. Grabbing the mouse, she scrolled down the page. "Oh my, God, are you illegal?" I stopped breathing for a second. I didn't know whether to answer or not. I wanted to tell her it was none of her business. I wanted to say that I simply forgot what a social security number was. *Was that even a thing*, I thought?

"Yes," I accidentally admitted.

"I'm sorry," is all she said to me. *Sorry*, what a horrible word. My world began to spin. I felt dizzy and confused. *The Army*, I thought. At least, I was going to be with a friend. I could already imagine the two of us having a blast offshore.

"Then I'll do the army," I said proudly.

"I'm sorry, but," she started, but before she could finish, I stood up and was already headed out the door.

"Excuse me? Where are you going? You can't just leave school campus."

"Chinga tu madre," I yelled furiously. I grabbed a textbook from a shelf and threw it at the whiteboard. She stood there too petrified to say anything else.

***

I put the last screw in and missed the stud. The drill gun disappeared behind the wall.

"Voy al baño," I yelled pulling the gun back. With my face covered in sweat and drywall powder, I needed some fresh air. I wiped my forehead with the back of my hand, I could hear Clayton yelling from a distance.

"You gon'ne mo' to wipe da dirt off yo skin," Clayton yelled.

"It's just drywall powder!" I yelled back.

"I'm talkin' bout dat skin, boy," Clayton chucked showing off all his missing front teeth. I returned my half smile but frowned remembering how Hope didn't like it when I gave it. I made my way outside and walked towards the van where I took a quick piss. Feeling an itch on the tip of my nose, I wiped my face again.

"Mijo," Rocky yelled. Sitting on the street curb, Rocky was puffing on a cigarette as he looked across at another house being build.

"Sit," Rocky said calmly. "Read this for me." He handed me a small bag. "Es pa el cuerpo?"

"Yea, it's for body pain," I said reading the label.

"Sit down. Just for a minute," he suggested again as he noticed me getting ready to walk away.

Rocky never did anything. Every morning he would come to work and for the first couple hours he would pick some trash up and maybe patch a hole, but he mostly spent his time wondering off. I always wondered why he didn't just retire and stay home until it dawned on me that he couldn't. Like every illegal immigrant, he had nowhere to call home. He had been living here for over forty years, having grandchildren, and having adapted to the American lifestyle, I didn't think he could ever go back to a place he no longer knew. He admitted, at times, that he had grown a love for work. It wasn't the labor, but the people. I never really understood what he meant.

I wasn't the type to sit down and have a chat. I knew that if Clayton ever saw me slacking off, I'd be fired on the spot. *I need the money, not a good conversation*, I thought. Whenever Rocky called me over, he managed to get me to stop what I was doing. He would sit me down and ask me how everything was going. At times, I thought about telling him everything, but I always caught myself. I could tell that he knew I was lying because he never smiled like he did to the others, almost as if he felt sorry for me. Before I'd leave he'd always say, "Work hard and become someone or you'll end up like me. Old and lazy."

"I got to go back to work Rocky," I protested. "I think Juan is calling me. Really, I kinda just left 'em there."

"Sit! You work too much. Believe me, more than anyone I know," Rocky said.

I choked for a moment. I had been working for about a year now and every day I worked harder than the day before. Yet every day, Clayton would yell at how lazy I was.

"Don't listen to Clayton. He's crazy," Rocky grunted. I wanted to smile, but didn't. Instead, I sat down. I looked across the street. I could hear the workers and their hammering as they beat down nails onto the plywood. Someone yelled out the size of the next piece of plywood. Seconds passed, and I began to worry about being spotted by Clayton. I looked over at Rocky. He looked relaxed and without a care in the world.

"Boy, what in da hell are you doin'?" Clayton's yelled from behind me. I turned around ready to say something in my defense, but nothing came to mind. I got to my feet and stood frozen with my mouth slightly opened wanting to say something but nothing processed. Clayton's face was red with fury. He walked closer towards me. I could already hear him telling me to get my tools and leave.

"Lovely evenin' we havin'. Ain't it?" Rocky said.

"Yea, Rocky," Clayton said as the redness in his face disappeared. He took one last glance at me before walking away.

"I take pictures of anything that can get him in trouble. Unsafe ladders, scaffolds, and whatever," Rocky said.

"Blackmail?" I said, laughing inside. That's when Rocky handed me a piece of paper with his phone number. "I'm going to another company. Bigger pay but the catch is traveling all over. If you need a job after this project is over, call me. 'Cause you know how Clayton gets." I put the paper in my wallet on stood up. "Well, what you waiting on? Get back to work," Rocky shouted mimicking Clayton.

Not much was left of the house, but Clayton always liked finishing early so we could all go home. I didn't mind. I liked going home early. Sometimes it wasn't like that. At times, he would tell us to finish early, and he would drive to another house and threaten us that if we didn't finish it that day, he wouldn't pay us. I never worried because we always finished but when we didn't, he was serious. Even if it wasn't our fault. Even if we were out of materials he would say it wasn't his problem and that we should have done a better job. I thought about quitting like my brothers and father but never did. I stuck around. I had this idea of getting to know the trade and one day starting my own sheet-rocking company. It wasn't going to be easy, but I needed to start somewhere. Every day on the drive home, I asked Clayton something. Some days he was willing to answer my questions and other days he would tell me to shut the fuck up. That day I didn't bother to ask him anything since he had caught me sitting on my ass. I rode silently as he made his way to drop me off home.

When I got home, Grant was leaning against my old pickup truck. Clayton's beat down white van pulled into what was supposed to be a driveway but was a large patch of missing grass. Luckily, large enough for a car to pull in. I slid the van's door open and stepped out with my tool belt in one hand and my drill gun in the other.

"Orale, buey!" I yelled at everyone inside.

"Looks like you had a rough day," Grant asked.

"Nah, the drywall gets lighter every day," I replied with a warm smile. I dropped everything in my hands to shake his hand.

"Where you been, brother?" Grant said concerned.

"Nowhere really," I shrugged my shoulders. A squirrel in a tree caught my attention. I hoped I could hide my true feelings by watching it jump from branch to another.

"It's been nearly a year since the last time I saw or heard from you, brother. Since anyone heard from you" said Grant. I pulled the tailgate down so we could sit.

"Work," was all that could come out. It wasn't close to what was all actually going on in my mind. We looked at each other for a split second. He knew I was lying. I wondered if he looked at me differently since basic training. I wondered if he looked at me just as a friend, no more than the way you look at a stranger.

"Where you really been, brother?" Grant asked putting his hands in his pocket. I couldn't answer. I was too deep into thought. Then without realizing, I started talking.

"I can never be your brother. We could never grow the kind of bond that two soldiers grow." I looked at him, wanting to convince myself that we were still friends but I felt distant from him, from everyone. "I deserted all my friends because I'm angry at everyone but most of all. I'm furious with myself. I can never go to college or even join the army. I'm illegal. We're from different worlds. Just watching everyone around me. Just with that I get angry. Everyone's got a chance you know? Everyone's got a choice. I feel like I'm left with no choice, once again. I want to blame the system but.... The system wasn't designed for me. I get that. Why would their government fit my needs? It's my fault. Maybe I don't work hard enough, or maybe I'm not good enough."

"That's not true, brother."

I looked at him. *What does he know?* I thought. I've had to work ten hours a day trying to make the best I could with what I had just so I could have what they were already promised. Carefree and careless they all were, not afraid of life because, in the end, they would all leave and chase their dreams, with no one to stop them but their own doubt. But what is doubt to those who dream with passion and ambition? Nothing. They would all find happiness. Everyone but me.

"So, this is it, brother?"

"What do you mean, Grant?" That was the first time I ever called him by his name.

"I mean," Grant stopped, trying to find the right words. He scratched the top of his head. "This. Whatever this is. Are you happy I guess is what I'm tryna say."

"Yea," I said proudly. "I have everything I man can ever dream of. A great girlfriend and an all right paying job for an illegal immigrant. I mean even if I did want more," I said trying to hide the truth and the pain in me. "I'm illegal, remember? You know I can't do much," I paused. "So, yea, I'm happy."

"Well, I'm glad to hear that. But is Delilah really that great?"

"Every relationship has its bumps. We're having ours."

"So, you call cheatin' a bump?"

"Rumors," I interrupted.

"I ain't finished. A bump? So, when she sleeps with someone who she had just met at some party is a bump? Brother, why are you with her?" Grant looked into my eyes. I clearly had no answer. "I hear she's with Joe behind your back."

I looked away. Even if it was true, I couldn't leave Delilah. I couldn't go back to being alone in the world. Yea, maybe she was seeing someone else behind my back, but something kept her with me, so she must have still loved me or she would have left me for him a long time ago. Besides, they were only rumors. Not once had she acted as if she was actually doing anything behind my back and not once did I think about leaving her.

"Where is she anyways? Do you even know?" Grant asked ruthlessly. I didn't answer. "She's at Joe's," Grant answered for me.

"No, she's at her house. She's sick. I think a cold," I replied.

"Hmm," Grant pulled out his phone.

"What are you doing?" I asked.

"Hallah," answered a deep male voice. "Who dis?" he quickly asked.

"Umm," Grant said as he looked closely at the phone number, making sure he had the right number. "Is Delilah there," he requested.

"Yah, hey, Delilah, phone."

"Hey, is this Joe I'm talking to?" Grant asked.

"Yah, who dis?" Joe asked, but Grant quickly then hung up as if something important had come up. "Now, you call her."

"Nah."

"Call her," Grant demanded. I pulled out my phone and called her.

"Hey, baby," Delilah answered cheerfully.

"Hey, where are you right now?"

"I'm in my house getting ready for Joe's party. What about you? How was work?"

"It was ok."

"So, what's with the early phone call?"

"Just wanted to check up on you and your cold," I said. "You sure you should be going out tonight? Maybe, you can come over, and we can watch a movie."

"I would, baby. It's just that I've already promised Joe I would go. Tomorrow we can make plans."

"Oh, ok."

"Well, I got to go. See you tomorrow?"

"So, what are you going to do?" Grant asked as I hung up the phone.

"I don't know," I replied. My heart ached at the idea of Delilah loving someone else. "Come to Joe's party with me tonight."

Grant looked uncertain. "Alright," he said.

I walked to my front door. I thought back to the beautiful ranch home we once lived in. It was nothing compared to our new home. We had left the large wide open space of actual freedom and simple living to a small single wide mobile home. And the land around us, not that it was ours, was filled with bald spots only large enough to park the truck my father owned. The only thing he owned. It wasn't supposed to be like this.

When we had first moved in, my father had promised it was temporary until we found a bigger house. He would describe it with a beautiful front lawn and a pool in the back. That was the first and last time I ever saw my mother and father genuinely happy. Hope of a bright future had filled their hearts and I could see it all through their luminescent eyes. I could not wait for that day. I wanted to see them smile the way they did all those years ago. Years passed, and we never did move out. It never bothered me. I was grateful enough to be with my family and have a roof over our heads. Sometimes I thought about the house with the beautiful front lawn and pool in the back when my elbows brushed against the narrow hallway walls or as I crashed into my brother trying to get to the other side of the trailer. My father never gave up, though.

Even after he started receiving letters from the IRS declaring that he owed the government money, he kept his head up. He repeated his promise that, one day, we would have a front lawn. He made his best efforts to pay what he owed, but his debt never seemed to come to an end. We owned nothing, yet owed everything to everyone. I watched my parents work day in and day out. Being too young at the time, all I could do was work hard in school and hope that one day I'd get us all out the filth we were living in. But even that came to a screeching halt. In the end, I worked alongside my father and two brothers stacking bricks and sheet rocking residential homes, building the American Dream for others but never for ourselves. Every day, I noticed my father's glimmering light of hope being suffocated by a sense of failure. Sometimes, I would witness as he would stop whatever it was he was doing and look into the distance as if trying to convince himself that the silver lining was just up ahead. And whenever he noticed I was staring, he would turn my way and smile. It wasn't happiness thought. He was exhausted, ready to give up. My father had changed greatly and so had everyone else.

My father was fighting with the doorknob when I walked in. He was trying to open his bedroom door, which my mother had locked, and was now standing behind yelling. Seeing me come inside, my father came to his senses for a second before my mother yelled, "Me prometiste!"

I walked over, "Mama, abre la puerta!" I tried convincing her to open the door, but nothing I said convinced her. Tightly wrapping my fingers around the doorknob, I could feel a part of me dying. I could hear her pacing around the bedroom opening drawers and throwing clothing into a suitcase. *She had had enough*, I thought. She was upset that my father hadn't gone to work for about a week now.

"Ya no, amor. Ya no puedo. Ya. No salimos de lo mismo!" She was tired of being stuck in the same place as everyone else moved ahead in life. I felt horrible, feeling just as responsible as my father. "Ya no le echas ganas. Y yo ya me canse." A piece of glass broke from inside the room. Feeling disrespected, my father began trying to break through the door with his shoulder.

"Abre la pinche puerta!" my father's voice roared.

"Papa," I pleaded trying to calm him down. I looked back expecting to see my brothers, but they were still at work. They wouldn't arrive for another hour.

"Ya no. Ya no te amo." Just then she stopped pacing the room. "Ya no te amo," she said again. I didn't understand, after everything how could she no longer love my father. "Me prometiste una casa y una vida mejor! Me prometiste!"

"Si. Si. Mi amor," was all my father could say as he lowers his head.

"Ya no puedo. Está bien. Me voy."

"Una casa, pues, te la voy a dar," my father pleaded.

"No, ya no," my mother cried. Her voice was cracking as if she was crying. My eyes began to well up and my throat began to ache as if, any minute now, I would burst into tears. I reached over to the doorknob and tried turning it in frustration, but it remained locked. "Mama, abre la puerta," I begged. No answer. "Mama!" She started pacing around the room again as if looking for something important but never finding what it was exactly. That's when she walked up towards the door and told me.

"Hijo, vive tu vida pero cuando encuentras a alguien a quien amas, no hagas promesas que no puedes mantener."

———

I arrived at the party still shaken from what was going on in my house. I felt uneasy knowing my house was a mess, with my mother still locked behind the door I didn't feel comfortable leaving. What if something happened and I wasn't there? My mind was wrapped around the idea of returning to a shattered home. The entire drive I wanted to turn around but never did. I wanted to believe that love was worth nearly losing my family. I didn't even know what I was doing exactly, I just knew I felt that I needed to be here if I truly loved Delilah. Perhaps I was there to kick Joe's ass or maybe I was there to convince Delilah, once and for all, that I was the man she had always dreamed of. Maybe, it was both.

When I stepped out my truck, I was already being glanced at. I hadn't taken a shower and I was still wearing my work clothes. I didn't care. I wasn't there to party or to make friends. I was there for Delilah. Grant and I walked towards the large house when he noticed a group of girls in sundresses and, without knowing, split up in different directions. I searched for Delilah without a distraction until my eyes caught a familiar face. She wore a white band T-shirt with red stripes on it and jeans that were ripped all over. Her dark blonde hair covered most of her face, which was lit only by the cigarette that rested between her lips. Still, I recognized her.

"Hope?" I asked.

"Ally," the girl said as she inhaled her cigarette. In a burst of excitement, she tried to jump towards me for a hug. Instead, she bumped into me like a drunk maniac and landed on my chest. Hope leaned on my shoulder and blew smoke into my face, flicked the cigarette onto the floor, and then wrapped her arms around me. Breathing deeply, she whispered softly, "I missed you. Where have you been?"

"Hope?"

"Ally," she leaned in closer. That's when I smelled the alcohol. "I'm happy now." She stretched her arms into the air and reached around my neck. "Come on let's go be happy together." Without realizing it, I had pushed her off me.

"Ally. Ally. Ally," she started singing in a tune.

She came near me, stumbled and fell on my shoulder again. *I can't leave her here*, I thought.

"Come on, Ally. Let's party," she yelled. A crowd of people yelled as they rose their drinks to the sky. "Ally, I want you to meet Jesus Christ our lord and savior. Come on. Come on. I want you to meet Jesus. You know about our Lord and Savior, right?" She reached over my hand and dragged me across the street into Joe's house. A tall white man with a wild beard that reached down to his chest was standing next to a mailbox negotiating a price with two heavy-set guys who looked like they were part of the school football team.

Jesus? I wondered. Hope walked towards him and collapsed on the front lawn. She leaned on the mailbox and looked up at him with a face filled with admiration. The two football players were ready to leave when I noticed Delilah coming out the house. Joe followed her.

"You finally wanna try it?" I heard Jesus ask.

"My savior, please. Save me from everything," Hope said reaching her arms into the sky and embracing a force I couldn't see.

85

I was ready to walk towards Delilah, but I stopped as she reached over and placed her arms around Joe. I stopped to see what else was about to happen. Delilah looked into his eyes, gave him a blissful smile, and, getting on the tip of her feet, kissed him.

"Let's go, brother," I heard Grant saying behind me. He reached his hand over and gently squeezed my shoulder. "He's not worth it."

"That's it, though. He is. He's worth more than I could ever be." I said walking towards Joe and Delilah. Joe noticed me and stood in front of Delilah as if protecting her from me.

"Ey, man, she choosed meh," Joe said raising his hands in the air as if he had nothing to do with her disloyalty. I didn't care. I wasn't there for him. I had stretched my hand out towards Delilah when Joe's fist flew through the air and landed on my face. I stumbled back, almost falling to the ground. Blood fell into my mouth. I looked at Joe puzzled and scared at the same time. I hadn't been in a fight since I left my hometown. I didn't know what to do. I didn't know who to be.

"Alejandro!" Delilah yelled. "What are you doing here?"

"Back up, Bruh," Joe demanded as his surrendering hands now became trigger happy fists.

"What am I doing. What are you doing?" I screamed. A crowd of people flocked to see the action. We were surrounded. There was no escape for any of us.

"I need more, Alejandro," Delilah softly said, "and right now you're not enough for me."

"And he is!" I yelled looking at Joe, who still had his fists in the air. I looked Joe up and down and envied him. His house shined through the night and lit up like a castle. "What is it? Is it the money? What?" Delilah was ready to answer when I interrupted her. "Come home, Delilah, please?" I said completely ignoring what she had just said. I walked over to her again, when Joe jolted towards me and tackled me to the ground. I lost my breath. He laid on top me as he repetitively punched me in the face. I did nothing. I could hear Delilah yelling and the crowd of people cheering Joe on.

Grant was ready to charge in when someone grabbed him by the shirt and threw him back into the crowd. "Brother," he yelled.

"Stop it, Alejandro! I love him, not you. Stop it!" Delilah pleaded as she tightened her small hands into fists. Joe finally stood up. His fists were covered in my blood.

"You love him?" I asked.

"He's everything I've dreamed of, and you're just," she paused. She wanted to tell me the truth but wasn't sure.

"I'm what?"

"Yua punk! Yu po, no money. She want me. Rich and handsome," Joe's said, "an' not a broke illegal wetback who live in a shed." He laughed as everyone else joined in with him.

I felt a sting in my chest. I was ready to strike Joe when I felt someone pull on my arm. I looked back to see Grant holding trying to hold me back. I expected him to repeat what he had said earlier about how Joe wasn't worth it.

"You're better than him, brother," Grant said. *Was I really*, I wondered? No, I wasn't, I couldn't be. What did I have that could possibly make me better than Joe? Nothing, that's what. He had everything I could only dream of. He had money, a beautiful house, a bright future, and now Delilah. I wasn't better than him and I could never be. I looked away from Grant and looked at Delilah.

"So, you do love him?" I asked.

"Yes, I do!" Delilah yelled, frustrated with me. Joe had finally had enough and jolted toward me again. I gave him my half smile as everything went black.

Delilah's face wore the kind of look you only see in horror films. No one in the crowd was chanting anymore. Things had taken a turn down a road they had never been. Then, a smile appeared on her face, "You do love me. You would fight for me," she said. My fists were covered in blood, but I continued to beat on Joe's motionless body. There was a horrible silence when I stood up and stomped my foot on Joe's face. "You do love me," she said again. She reached over and grabbed my arm, but I shrugged her off. Giving her a disgusted look, I stormed off.

I had spent what felt like a lifetime trying to become a better person, someone kind and loving. Someone with a future. I had hoped that I could become someone worth loving. Now here I was being admired for the monster I once was. *How could she love a monster? What was wrong with the hardworking man I wanted to be?* I thought.

Delilah said something, but all I could hear was a loud ringing inside my head. I walked away. As the ringing died off, I could hear her calling after me. This wasn't what I had wanted or what I had come for. I pushed through the crowd. No one tried to stop me. I could feel them all staring at me like children at a zoo, fascinated but at the same time fearful and disgusted. Delilah was still calling after me when I got into my truck. I looked down the road then towards the crowd of people who were now rushing towards Joe, when I noticed someone stepping inside.

"Ally," Hope whimpered. Calmly, she came down and rested her head on my lap. I jerked back afraid of getting blood on her hair, but it was too late. "I missed you. A lot. Like, a lot a lot." She grabbed my hand and placed it on her head. I tried pulling it back, but she insisted that my bloody hand play with her tangled hair. "I love your truck. Reminds me of your story." Untangling her hair, she rubbed her face on my lap. "The one about the boy who rides around the neighborhood his girlfriend once lived in. It's such a sad story." I brushed down her tangled hair and thought of the story. I was surprised that she had remembered it. It was about a hopeless romantic that couldn't let go of the past, a simple and cliché story. "He drives and drives and drives and drives around the neighborhood in circles," Hope whispered. "Alone, trying to relive the past." My lap began to feel wet. A weak whimper came out of Hope, and that's when I realized she was crying. I rubbed her head, thinking it would ease her when an ambulance and cop pulled into Joe's driveway. Someone flew to the officer screaming and yelling. Everyone pointed in my direction. "You always had a way with words, Ally." The officer approached my truck. Flashing his lights inside he panicked seeing all the blood on my shirt and Hope laying on my lap like a dead corpse, I could only imagine what was going through his mind. "You have such a way with words, Ally," Hope mumbled. Looking down at Hope I wondered, *this can't be Hope.* I couldn't help but feel guilty, as if everything Hope had gone through was entirely my fault. She had done so much for me. How could I be so cruel and abandon her in the world I grew to know as dark and empty? She was lost and hurt, and it was all my fault.

"Get out of the vehicle!" a cop yelled. It wasn't long before he was dragging me out and shoving my face on the concrete floor. More officers showed up and beat me savagely before putting me in the back seat of a cop car. I sat there for a short period before an officer stepped inside and began writing something on his notepad.

"Don't worry. I'ma let your parents know. Everything's gonna be Ok!" Grant yelled from a distance.

"What's your full name," said the cop loudly. He had a heavy voice, the kind of voice that doesn't know what whispering is. I kept my mouth shut, not a word came out. "That's fine. Either way, I got more than enough information from your friends." He dropped his notepad and began typing on a laptop that rested on the passenger seat. "Hmm, you not coming up. You an American citizen?" He asked harshly. "Do you have documentation?" yelled the cop. Aggravated, he looked back at me and stared me down as he waited for me to respond.

"I'm not, Officer," I finally answered ashamed. I looked away trying to avoid feeling guilty. He closed his laptop and watched as Joe was being put in an ambulance. He pulled off just as the ambulance did. The entire ride nothing was said between us. I kept my eyes on him in an attempt to read his mind. I wondered what he thought about me. I wasn't a bad kid. I wanted him to know that, but there was nothing I could say that could change what he already thought of me. I would imagine starting a conversation by asking for his name and if he had a family. Then, maybe, we would joke about how our jobs suck but we do it for our families so it was all worth it. After our short conversation, I imagined him turning around with a smirk on his face and saying, "You're not a bad kid after all." It rendered perfectly in my mind, but just as I was ready to open my mouth I would stop myself because, even if I did change his image of me, that wasn't going to change the fact that I was going to jail.

I kept my mouth shut the entire ride up to the large building surrounded by barbed wire fences. I lost more faith every time we passed a checking point. Inside the building, the cop took his cuffs off me and guided me into a room where there were three other people sitting on metal benches waiting to be booked. They looked at me at with horror as my shirt was covered in blood and my face looked like it was used as a punching bag. Scared and cautious, they both stared at me as I went to the farthest bench in the room to sit alone. I looked down at my hands thinking, *well, this is what you get.*

"Ally, Ally, Ally, Ally!" I soon heard a voice singing. It was a child-like melody. I looked up. Hope was being brought in by another police officer. Her hair was now in a ponytail and her eyeliner was smeared down her face. She skipped my way and made herself comfortable next to me.

"Damn, it looks like Joe did a number on you," Hope said examining my face.

"Yea, really?" I said ignoring her comment and, as much as possible, tried not to talk about the incident. I wasn't proud of what I had just done. I looked away. Embarrassed and ashamed, I couldn't look at Hope. I was afraid she would see me the way everyone else did.

"I saw the fight. I'm glad you stood up for yourself, Ally. Joe's a prick," Hope said with a laugh. Then, she continued her sweet child-like tune.

"You should have came with me and smoke some weed. Weed makes everything better," Hope suggested in the middle of her tune. "Ally, Ally, Ally, Ally, Ally, Ally, Ally, Ally, especially in times like this, Ally." She took in a deep breath. "You feel funny? It's kindah hard to breathe in here."

I shrugged my shoulders and watched the cops pass papers around. I was still ignoring Hope, trying not to show my distorted face to her. "I'm going to have a great time here, Ally. You know. Before they arrested me, Jesus gave me some magic stuff. Smooth sailing." I glanced at her trying to figure out what she meant. "Man, I feel so warm and cozy." Hope stretched her arms around and wrapped herself like a blanket. "When we get out, Ally. Let's go see Jesus Christ together." She leaned against the wall looking up at the ceiling tile and dazed out. I thought about what she meant, and it bothered me. I had an idea as to what she was inviting me to, I felt bothered by it. I couldn't see Hope, even as she sat right in front of me, as a junkie. I didn't want to. Looking at her and seeing her bloodshot eyes and ruined make-up, I lied to myself. She was just tired. Then, her lips began to look unnaturally blue. I told myself it was lip gloss. She took another deep breath then sighed. "Ally, I'm tired." Hope yawned, then closed her eyes. I yawned right after her. She fell into a deep sleep when I realize her breathing was shallow almost as if she was out of breath. I had seen this before. My heart dropped, and my palms got sweaty as I anticipated what was about to happen. I sat there staring at Hope not knowing what to do. All I could do was pray and lie to myself that nothing was wrong, that she was fine and that my mind was playing mind tricks.

"Ryan Bob Blourde," yelled an officer. I glanced around until finally someone got up and walked towards the officer. He looked like a body builder. I wondered what he had done to get arrested and if there was any struggle between him and the officers. I watched as the body builder took his mugshot and was led into another side of the building. As he disappeared through a set of double doors, Hope's cheek fell onto my shoulder then down my chest. I was ready to catch her when she collapsed without warning into the floor. I panicked and quickly rose to my feet. A cop noticed and also panicked.

"Get back in your seat," he demanded.

"She needs help," I shouted back. I approached the cop, forgetting that I was a criminal with a distorted face and blood covered shirt. The cop panicked.

"Get back to your seat!" the cop yelled trying to scare me and at the same time gain the attention of his partner, who was looking through some paperwork.

"She needs help, you fuckin' pig!" He tried pushing me back into the room. I heard his partner calling for more policemen. I looked back at Hope. She was still on the ground breathing unnaturally when all of a sudden, her body lay motionless. I jolted back to her.

"Hope!" I pleaded. She wasn't breathing. "Hope, Hope!" I called out to her, trying my best not to lose control. I looked back at the officer, hoping that he had realized what was going on and that he would call for help, but he hadn't. Instead, he continued demanding that I get back to my seat. "She needs help."

Tears escaped my swollen face. I could see through the look in his eyes what he thought about Hope because it was the same look I had been given my entire life. Hope was just another druggy who ran out of luck and finally overdosed. But she wasn't; she was filled with inspiration and a passion for finding happiness. Out of all the people I've met in my life, she was the one out of the many that needed to live. More officers arrived and roughly grabbed me. Instinctively, I fought back and grew furious that none of them bothered to help Hope. I was dragged out the room, leaving Hope alone. I needed to go back to her. Pushing an officer off, I saw an opportunity as he stumbled backward. I tackled him to the ground, reached over to his belt, and grabbed his gun.

"Put the weapon down!" an officer demanded as I pointed the gun at him and then at another officer who I was attempting to approach me.

"Help her," I pleaded as tears poured down my bruised face. "Please." I looked over at Hope.

"Put the weapon down," another officer demanded in a gentler tone. I looked at the officer and pointed the gun at him. He looked scared. This was probably the first time he had seen someone point a gun at him.

"Please," I said. I looked down at the gun. *It's over*, I thought. *My life is over. What life? To live, I needed to exist. I don't even exist in this country.* So many thoughts raced through my mind, I couldn't keep up with all of them, but I knew how I felt. And I felt useless because even with Hope just a couple feet away I couldn't help her. I felt sick at my own existence.

"Put the gun down," demanded another police officer.

It's over, I thought. *I might as well shoot myself.* I pulled the gun back and aimed it at my head. I was ready to pull the trigger when everything went dark.

Chapter XI

April 21, 2011
Fear no man for all are flesh and blood

The door behind me rattled. No one entered. A janitor looked inside, and then walked away. I stared out the small window and watched inmates pass by. A cop eventually barged in like a madman and dragged me out to take my mug shot. Another officer stood behind him, cautiously watching over me as he gripped his pistol. Neither one ever got the handcuffs off me. I tried my best to not look in their direction and only looked up when told.

"Look straight. Look left. Look right."

My father picked up when I finally got my free phone call.

"Como andas?" he asked.

"Bien," I responded.

"Dios tiene un plan para todo, bueno o malo."

"Y mi ama?" I asked. He didn't respond. He coughed. He was ready to say something when I lied and told him my time was up. I wasn't ready for whatever it was he was going to tell me. I had to hang up. If she had left, I didn't want to know. Hopeless, I carried myself to the far back of the cell and thought about what my father said, "God has a plan for everyone, Good or bad," and wondered what God was planning for me.

Pressing my back up against the wall, I curled up into a ball. I thought about Hope and a sense of guilt came over me. I tried to shake it off. There was nothing I could have done to save her. Nothing. I knew this, and yet I had acted so stupidly. I tossed and turned but never found that one spot that felt comfortable. I turned to face the wall. With my nail, I scratched off the thin paint and drew a face. I needed some company in the empty cell room, the kind that doesn't say a word and doesn't mind sharing solitude. Then out of nowhere a shockwave ran up my spine. I felt a sharp pain on my side. I panicked and quickly turned around expecting someone. I was breathing heavy. Blood rushed to my face. I couldn't help but look in every direction, paranoid. I was on the edge. Almost losing my breath, I gripped my shirt. I starting searching for my empty pockets where I always kept a knife.

***

The flock of hens scattered frantically when I entered their den. One flew over my head and before another could run through my legs, I grabbed it by the neck and lifted it off the ground. I carried it over to the table. Pressing down on its body I took the machete and, without hesitating, chopped off its head. His body jerked and kicked. I looked at its eyes as they frantically looked everywhere, I guess trying to understand what had just happened. In seconds, the table was covered in blood. I was about ready to dunk it into the tank when my father showed up. The look in his eyes told me everything before his mouth did. Handing him the headless chicken, I listened to him explain how an eight-year-old wasn't old enough to be working with boiling water.

"Eres demasiado joven. Te quemarás." I guess one thing was killing an animal and another thing was working with dangerous equipment. He grabbed the chicken and dunked it into the scalding tank. I looked over to my older brother Luis, who was running a machete into a pig. It squealed one last time before dropping dead. I couldn't wait. I had been craving pork chops for some time now.

That night, Luis decided to take me into town. I guess he thought I was old enough to hang out with him now. I didn't act surprised, I acted cool and tried not showing off my excitement as Luis, his friends, and I all loaded up in the back of a pickup truck while my father was asleep.

Everything was disgusting and chaotic when we got to town. Kids no older than me were running around with spray cans painting, "33," on the walls. A homeless man laid on the street floor as a rat rushed out from the darkness and into his winter jacket. I noticed a syringe stuck on his arm and wondered if he was dead. Everyone in the truck starting yelling and whistling when we came across a prostitute standing in the corner of a street. Someone threw a beer can at her. She grabbed a rock from the ground and threw it back at us. Missing, she spat in our direction. Everything I thought about the rest of the world was not how I imagined it. We drove until the spray-painted walls started saying, "El Club de Billar." We stopped in front of a billiards night club. Tito was inside waiting. He was a middle-aged hardheaded easy tempered gang leader of The Pool Table Club. When I walked inside, he was beating someone with a pool stick. Everyone pretended to not notice as they look in other directions.

"Nico. Nico. Nico. Nico," Tito said until the pool stick finally broke in half. He picked up the two pieces of sticks and threw them out the window. Making a swinging motion with his hand, the beaten body was thrown out. That's when he noticed me, grabbed a knife sitting on a table, and started walking in my direction. I didn't move. I wasn't afraid of him, and I wasn't stupid. I had walked in with my hands in my pockets, already tightly gripping my pocket knife. I was relieved when he walked past me towards the door. That's when a sharp pain came to my side, and an electrical shockwave ran up my spine as Tito whispered in my ear, "It's better to have your back up against the wall." Everyone panicked when I instinctively pulled out my pocket knife and, in an uppercut motion, tried running my blade into the bottom of his jaw. The very tip of my blade managed to pierce him before Luis pulled me by my shirt. The cut on my side wasn't a serious wound, nothing that could have killed me. A simple bandage was enough. But had I managed to cut into Tito's jaw and slice his tongue, he probably would have bled to death. He didn't seem to mind that I had almost killed him. He thought it was funny. Seeing him barbarically beat someone to death, I had expected the same being done to me. Instead, he whistled and patted me on the head saying that one day I'd grow up to be just like him. I looked at everyone not knowing if that was a compliment or not.

Tito was a loose canon. I don't think there was ever a time where he was actually happy about something or wasn't beating someone or something down. Usually, after breaking the pool stick, he would feel more at ease, but sometimes it wasn't enough. Storming out the club, he would walk straight into 33 territory and start a fist fight with the first gang member he saw. In a matter of seconds, a gang fight would break out as everyone joined in. Even me. It's not like I had a choice. I didn't find comfort or pleasure in grabbing others, slamming them on the curb, and stomping their faces in. I just knew if I didn't move quickly enough my face was going to be slammed up against a brick wall as ten others beat me with bats and chains.

Besides his anger issues, he never let it get in the way of his actual responsibility. He was an ambitious man, with operations ranging from money laundering, extortion, prostitution, human trafficking, and drug dealing. Whether it was kidnapping someone for ransom, collecting money, or selling socks dipped in roofing adhesive to drug addicts, I never saw a problem with what we did. With no one to tell me all the wrong doing I was committing, I never saw the evil in my actions.

But it wasn't always like that. Sometimes when there wasn't anything to do, Tito would be teaching me how to play billiards. At first, I didn't think it was a good idea that someone with anger issues teaching me. I imagined getting beat up if I didn't learn quick enough, but he never did. He was patient with me. Whenever I messed up, he would laugh hysterically and suggest what I could do to improve. And when he saw me improving, landing shots even he couldn't do, he would whistle, pat me on my head, and tell me that one day I'd grow up to be just like him. In the middle of our games, he would talk to me about the importance in warfare or how much he hated Nico and his father. "Pinche perros!" he would curse at how, no matter how many times he tried, he couldn't get a single hair in either of their head. He needed both of them gone if he really wanted to expand his business in narcotics. He had so much ambition but, just like that, Tito was gone. I wasn't bothered by it because death was the only thing waiting for him and everyone else in this lifestyle. I guess death was the only actual goal; everything else like fame, glory, money, and power were just something to pass the time. To risk everything while you still could. Tito knew that, and I knew that.

Had it been luck or Nico's careful planning it didn't matter. Tito was gone. Without him, the town quickly became a war zone as El Club De Billar was being taken over. With no one to lead the club, it fell apart. Nico finally had complete control. He would walk around with his pistol tightly shoved in his pants and taunt everyone he crossed paths with. Even without bodyguards, no one stood up to him. I didn't care. Nico could do whatever he wanted as long as my family was left alone.

———

"No!" someone screamed. I was coming back from the plaza when I heard a girl yelling for help and pleading someone to stop. I walked over to see Nico with his pants unbuckled and hovering over a girl who had fallen to the floor in desperation. Her dress was ripped and was barely hanging on her shoulders. Laying on the ground, she covered her face and began crying. Countless pedestrians just walked by, afraid to do anything. I was too, I just stood there watching as he began kicking the girl in anger and frustration. He looked over at me with his bloodshot eyes and grinned. I walked away as he pulled out a bag of cocaine and his house key. No one did anything, not even the young girl's family. I didn't blame them. What could they do? As more girls started showing up beaten and even dead, everyone turned the other way.

I couldn't do the same when my brother Luis came home almost beaten to death. That same day I found Nico. And in broad daylight I sliced his throat. I reached over and grabbed his pistol and before anyone could realize what had happened, I was gone.

I don't know what it is about powerful men that makes them believe they are untouchable and godlike but after killing Nico I discovered he was just flesh and bone. He had been made into this fictional character that could not be touched by anyone. Yet in a matter of seconds, I had taken his life. So, what was it about his father that everyone treated him like a king and feared him like a God? Right after killing Nico I knew I had to kill his father. I walked over to their home pretending to be the new farm keeper. After feeding the horses, the guards didn't question me as I walked to the kitchen for a glass of water. Aimlessly wandering the house, I found his father's riches. There is was, millions of American dollar bills all stacked nicely next to a bed. Some bills laid scattered on the floor. I walked over and grabbed a hundred-dollar bill from the floor. I felt disappointed and amused at how this flammable piece of paper made him believe he was sort of God. Honestly, I had expected something more divine to explain the power he had. I puffed on a cigar that was on an ashtray on top the bed and tossed it into the money. I watched as it caught fire and Nico's father barged in. I had my gun ready, or rather Nico's gun, and before he could reach for his, I had already unloaded the entire magazine into his skull. I had won a war before it even started. I dropped the gun and with my arms over my head I stormed out. His guards rushed in, ignoring me and the idea that a child was responsible. From that moment on I came to understand that all men are made of flesh and bone. I would fear no man but God.

Chapter XII

April 23, 2011

God is good and evil

After forty-eight hours in a holding cell, my name was called. A smile came over my face. *Just like that,* I wondered as the cop called other names out. We all made a line and were led into a shower room. I wasn't being released as I thought. I was being processed into population. At least I was finally going to be able to wash the dry blood off my face. Putting on a faded out green outfit we made our way deeper into the jail. Walking through countless doors, I was finally led to a door with an eight on top.

The building had two floors and a large desk on the way in. An intercom and a laptop sat on top of a wooden table. I looked at my new home. On both sides of the building, there was a set of stairs that led to the cell rooms on the second floor. Two televisions were placed on opposite sides of the building. Blacks and whites circled around one of the television as all the Hispanics hovered closely as a commentator gave a play-by-play description of a soccer game. I tried listening to who was playing, but another officer stepped in front of my view. I tried looking past his shoulder, but it made no difference.

"Ok," he said taunting the new row of inmates. "I am in charge, your boss, and for the next remaining days you are here, the law. I am the one standing between you and freedom. You will do as I say and if you don't, it won't matter because, at the end of the day, I get to go home." He had a strong voice. I glanced at the officer and his badge. It read, "Johnson." I looked at him. I couldn't find a smirk, smile, frown, or anger on his face. Officer Johnson noticed and made his way towards me. "Understood?" he said leaning into my face. I nodded in a way that didn't show fear or bravery. I think he got the gesture because he walked away without saying a word. He started listing out rules and the times of when we were allowed out and when were expected back in our cells. I didn't listen to anything he said. They were all common-sense rules. *Just do as you're told and everything will go peachy*, I thought. Then he said something that struck me. "Everyone is expected to shower on a daily basis. If it becomes a problem, we are not scared to use force." I tried imagining someone who didn't like to shower and having to be forced by a whole team of policemen. I wondered if Officer Johnson had run into this problem before.

One by one, Officer Johnson showed everyone to their room. My room number was forty-eight. The room was four feet wide and eight feet long. The bed and toilet took up most of the space so there wasn't any actual room. I was relieved knowing I had no roommate.

"Make yourself home, kid," Officer Johnson said. I couldn't tell if he was being kind or sarcastic. I settled in and out of boredom I grabbed a towel and went to the showers.

"Youngblood, washu doin' time fo?" asked the voice of an elderly man as I entered the shower stall.

"Ummm, driving without a license," I said. I knew it wasn't the full truth. I knew I was in here for more than driving without a license, but I didn't want to share. Beating someone to death wasn't something I was really proud of. The elderly man didn't say anything. Instead, he let out a grunt, the kind that elder men do.

"Youngblood, you'll be outta here in ina. Ina day or two. You here! A day or two." The man sounded well over his fifties, and it got my curiosity running. I wondered what a man of that age could have done to be in jail.

Turning on the shower head, I ran my fingers down my face. I felt bruises and cuts. It wasn't bad, but it could have been avoided. "What are you in here for?" I asked.

"Fo bein' a man." With that, our conversation ended. I finished my shower and putting back the same shaded green outfit, I stepped out and leaned over the balcony. I could hear arguing and the voices of men demanding someone to cooperate.

"Hey, hey, sweetheart. Come on now, sugarplum. Be gentle." The husky man had an old New Yorker accent. "Hey, how you doin', Officer Johnson? I'm glad seeing you. How's the wife and kids?" Officer Johnson did not respond. "That's good to hear. No news is good news, right? Anyways, could you tell your guys to be a bit more gentle? You wouldn't want me to file domestic abuse now, would you?" I decided to step into my cell. Whatever was about to happen was none of my business. Inside, I jumped on top of the bunk bed and listen as the New Yorker got louder and louder. I looked up and through the cell window. He was being pushed up the stairs.

Please God, not my room, I thought. The officers and inmate walked past my cell. I sighed.

"Hey, it's this room. Bring him over here," I heard an officer yell. My cell door was being opened. *Fuck*, I though. After savagely pushing the man inside, the officers quickly closed the door and stormed out. The man stumbled in but didn't fall. Regaining his balance, he dusted his county jail shirt.

"Fuckin' wise guys. They don't know who they're messing with." I laid back down and tried to make it seem that I was asleep, but I could tell he was looking straight at me. "Ayy, I got a new roommate!" He yelled in excitement. I couldn't pretend I hadn't just heard his loud voice. I pretended to have been waking up from a nap. I rubbed my eyes.

Without warning, he yelled, "What's your name, kid?"

"Alejandro," I said giving a fake yawn.

103

"Nice name, kid. Name's Johnny. Man, it's good being back in my cell."

"This was your room already," I said unintentionally.

"Yea," Johnny said. "What you in here for, kid?"

"Driving with no license."

"Kid, you'll be outta of here tomorrow. Forget about it," Johnny said sitting on the bottom bed.

"I don't think so," I said.

"Why is that, kid?" asked Johnny.

"Well, hopefully, by tomorrow, immigration will come, pick me up, and deport me. I don't wanna stay here more then I should."

"Your illegal, kid?" Johnny said rubbing his forehead in disbelief.

"So, what you do?" I said trying to avoid being the center of attention.

"I'm in the market. I sell products that the American people can't live without."

"Like toilet paper."

"Kid, you think I'd be in jail for selling ass wipes? I sold," Johnny stopped and looked at the ceiling then scratched his head. "Drugs, kid, I sold drugs." Johnny stood up, then walked over to the toilet to take a piss.

"Drug dealer?"

"Yeup," Johnny said looking over his shoulder to give me a childish grin. "Someone got to do it. You think selling drugs is a bad thing, huh? No, leaving your mom, your dad, and your family penniless, homeless, and hungry is bad. It's not how you make the money that matters really. It's how you spend it that counts. I've done more terrible things than selling drugs to feed empty stomachs." He stopped to zip his pants up. "They don't care what I sell, kid. Trust me when I say this. They need me selling this shit. Without me and the business I do, a quarter of Americans would be out of a job, maybe even half. What drug trafficking, what violence, what prison cells? No more cops, probation officers, DEA, Officer Johnson, rehabilitation centers the lists goes on, kid. They need me. I make a mess, and they'll gladly pick it up. Of course, for a good salary and a bonus every other month cause we all know little Suzy wants that new dress for homecoming. But don't get me wrong. The moment people start buying bubble gum more than cocaine, I'll gladly switch over." He flushed the toilet before continuing. "Kid, honestly this isn't how I imagined my life to turn out but there is only so little a man can give and so much he can take. One day you'll understand and when you do kid, you'll see things differently." He sat back down on the bed. "You graduate kid. I hear if you finished high school you won't get deported."

"No, I wish I did."

"Forget about it," Johnny said taking his slippers off. "There's only one place you'll actually get an education. Jails just like these anyways. I'm not lying to you kid. Take it from me. You find something money can't buy. You find," he paused and looked up at the ceiling again. "Philosophy, kid. It's for the poor cause they can't afford an education. The hopeless 'cause it'll make you believe in something when you got nothin'. The imprisoned. 'Cause as long you can think you'll always be free." He stopped to look at me. "I'm tell you somethin' else kid. Behind these walls, I learned what it was to be more than a man. Kid, there are two things in this world, bad people and good people." I had never met someone who talked as much as Johnny. "It's like the Ying-Yang shit the Japanese or Vietnamese people believe in. And there is that circle, the orb, the thing holding them together. You gotta be that, kid. Good people ain't bad. And bad people ain't good. You gotta be able to be both, kid. If you wanna be more than just a man. We're good and bad remember that kid. I've done bad shit to do good things and good things for bad reasons."

Someone virtuous and evil. An individual who simply was, I thought. It all sounded God-like.

"Ten minutes before lights out," yelled Officer Johnson.

"I like you, kid. You know why?" he asked finally crawling into bed.

"No, why?" I asked concerned for my well-being. I had always heard about being raped in jails and wondered if this is how it happened.

"I saw you defend that girl when I was being sent away," Johnny said seriously. "You managed to steal a cop's fuckin' gun." He laughed. "You got some balls, kid." Johnny laughed hysterically recalling the incident. "Man, I would have shit my pants seeing all those guns pointed at me."

"She died," I said. Johnny stopped laughing.

"Sorry to hear that, kid." Johnny asked as the lights went off. "How you know?"

"I've seen enough to know."

"Did you know her? Was she your goyl or something?"

"No, just a close friend," I replied softly. Turning over on my side, I tried not thinking about Hope.

"I like you, kid," Johnny said again. "You know immigration it probably going to show up tomorrow and take you in," Johnny said concerned.

"Yea, well wish me luck and maybe I can get a loan from someone to come back," I said with a light laugh.

"Kid, if you weren't to get deported and instead were released tomorrow. Where would you go and do? Like what's your dream?"

No one had ever asked me that question. I didn't know whether to answer it or not but seeing that I was probably never going to see Johnny I decided to answer his question honestly.

"I guess seeing my situation I can't have much. But I've never wanted money. I don't want fame or fortune. I grew up on a farm in Mexico, you know. Some small town called Monte Sierra. My father taught me to work for what's necessary. I guess I don't want to go to college anymore. So, I guess. I want to be around people I can love even if they don't love me. Marry a woman, love her deeply. Have children. Watch them grow out of my arms," I paused. "What more could I ever dream of?"

"I like that answer. You should of been a writer," Johnny replied. "You said Monte Sierra?"

"Yea Monte Sierra. Honestly, I thought it sounded pretty corny," I said grinning.

"Nah, kid."

I couldn't tell if seconds, minutes, or hours passed but the silence felt like forever. I didn't know if Johnny was a silent sleeper so it was impossible to tell if he was asleep. I kind of wanted to start a conversation out of boredom, but I didn't want to wake him if he was asleep. I tossed and turned thinking about what I had said. Did I really mean it? I tried imagining myself with a family, a wife and children. It did sound pretty good. Although I knew Delilah wasn't in my future, I still imagined her sitting in the living room. A child or two would run to her, and I would sit next to them. It played so well in my head.

"Hey, kid," Johnny said out of the darkness.

"Hmm," I said still trying to focus on the image.

"How's your brother Luis," Johnny asked.

"Fine," I answered. I stopped to think back to our conversation and wondered had I mentioned anything about my family.

"I did business in Monte Sierra with a wise guy named Tito. Now that I think about it, he talked about you a lot. Said you was smart." Hearing Tito's name startled me. I couldn't help but feel threatened in the room. I pretended to not have heard his comment, but he continued. "A fuckin' kid. Even I couldn't believe it. No one did. I knew. You did me a big favor. That Pablo Enerma was rising prices on shitty product, threatening my business. I was gonna do it myself but just as I walked out my front door. I hear him and his kid were killed. No one knew and no one would believe a kid did it. I did. I did. Now here we are. Like God, kid. I don't believe in coincidence."

"I don't know what you're talking about," I protested. I grew paranoid. I couldn't trust him. He knew about what I had done and even if he sounded like he was on my side I didn't know his true intentions.

"Don't play stupid with me kid. I know, trust me. You can't trick a trickster. I did imagine you being a lot different though."

That morning, Johnny quickly stormed out during breakfast and made a phone call using Officer Johnson's personal cell phone. The entire time I ate, I kept my eyes on him and anyone that made any sudden movement. If anything was going to happen, I wanted to be ready. But out of everyone I kept my eyes close on Johnny. I watched him as he talked on the phone. I wondered who he was talking to. That's when Johnny turned around and raised his hand. Waving it towards me, I walked over. I managed to heard the last bit of his conversation.

"Yea, Ms. Emerson. Thank you. I'll make sure God himself opens the pearly gates for you," Johnny stopped. "Yea, Yea. He's a good kid. We owe him, and when he's ready, he won't say no. It's in his blood. It's his fate. Grazie. Arrivederci," Johnny said as he finally hung the phone and returned it to Officer Johnson.

"You Italian?" I asked trying to seem unaffected by what he said last night.

"No, but that doesn't mean I shouldn't learn another language. The world's moving fast kid. You gotta keep up."

"You ready to go?" Officer Johnson then asked me.

"Yea," I replied confused.

"Hey, kid, name one of your kids after me and we'll be even," Johnny yelled. "Johnny Giovanni! It's got a ring to it, don't it?" Walking out the door, I could hear him yelling, "Agghh, forget about it, kid!"

Chapter XIII

"Who were the Knights of Templar?" asked Professor Luther. Anthony looked over at Josh. He was looking at him with the same expression. "Anyone know?"

"They were soldiers who defended pilgrims headed to the holy land. Who later established a banking system," explained a student from the back.

"More or less," Professor Luther said. Anthony glanced at Josh again, who now seemed mildly interested in the topic. "What was their downfall?" he asked. Professor Luther was ready to start when he was interrupted by the same student.

"Some king in France believed they were becoming too powerful and had most of them burned at the stake." Anthony looked back curious to know who he was going to befriend if he wanted to pass Professor Luther's class. To his surprise, it was the same guy that had gotten Persela's phone number. He could not remember his name, but his face was enough to upset him. Marc noticed Anthony staring him down. He raised his middle finger and pointed it towards Anthony. Blood rushed to his head. Had he seriously just given him the finger? He tightened his grip causing his pencil to snap.

"Well, damn. I guess that's good," Josh said chuckling at Marc's answer.

"And why is that?" asked Professor Luther. Waiting for a response, his eyes widened. Josh thought about what he was going to

111

say but could not bring himself to saying it. He wanted to express his opinion and explain that no organization should grow to large, but before he could open his mouth, he stopped.

"I mean," Josh started. "Fuck 'em," he said then broke out in laughter. Everyone joined in the hysteria. Professor Luther anticipation vanished.

Professor Luther returned to lecturing the class. Secretly, Josh was interested in everything the professor had to say about the Knights' history. He found it all interesting. *Who were they really*, he wondered as his professor continued.

"What the matter?" Josh asked Anthony when they stepped out the classroom.

"I don't fucking like that guy," Anthony said. Josh looked out to the hallway but could not tell who he was referring to, so he changed the topic.

"So, Helene and Persela were talking about going to a new hookah bar that just opened." He looked over. Anthony was still fixated at Antonio as he continued grating his teeth. "I think it's called Up in Smoke, or something like that," Josh said trying to ignore the noise he made with his teeth. "What's the matter?" Josh asked again. Anthony continued. Josh snapped. Realizing who Anthony was staring at, Josh approached Marc from behind. Walking behind him, he grabbed his tightly wrapped backpack and led him into a bathroom. Marc jerked side to side but wasn't able to free himself. Josh tossed him up against the wall but instead Marc fell to the floor and squirmed around like a turtle on his back. Josh picked him up and threw him into an empty stall. Marc stood up and before he could say anything Josh swung at his ribs. Marc coughed as his lungs deflated. He hunched over in pain.

"I don't ever want you near my girl, and if I catch you near her I'll ruin your fuckin' life," Anthony demanded over Josh's shoulder. Catching his lost breath, Marc looked up at them.

112

"Fuck you. Both of you," Marc said with the bit of air he had. Marc noticed Josh's eyes beginning to turn red. A smirk grew on Marc's face. Furious, Josh punch him again.

"Say another fucking word," Josh said. He reached over and grabbed Marc by his shirt and lifted him off his feet.

"What? You too scared to do your job as a boyfriend? You have to get others to do it for you?" Marc said looking over Josh's shoulder towards Anthony. "Look at you. Are you scared?" Marc said then laughed hysterically. "And you should be more yourself and not what others think of you," he said looking back at Josh.

"Fuck 'em," he said mocking Josh. "I can't believe you said that! Fuck 'em!" he continued laughing. "Fuckin' moron!" Josh's and Anthony's faces went pale in embarrassment. They didn't know how to respond. Not knowing what to do, Josh savagely pushed Marc towards the toilet stall.

"You don't know who I am," Josh said in a shaky voice.

"I don't need to," Marc replied. Josh lost control and began kicking and punching Marc. It wasn't long before Anthony joined. The bell rang. They stopped and came to a halt like boxers at the end of a round. They looked down at Marc, who was motionless in fetal position.

"We need to get to class," Josh insisted. "I mean you need to get to class. Um. Um. Um. I'ma go. I have to see him." Ready to storm out, Josh grabbed Anthony by his shirt but Anthony shrugged him off.

"Who's weak now, huh? Answer me, you piece of shit. Who's weak and small? You fuckin' piece of shit. I'm the fuckin' Omega," he said kicking Marc. "I'm fucking God." Anthony kicked him one last time. For the first time, Anthony felt what it meant to stand over someone. It was a feeling like no other.

Josh didn't see anyone in the hallways when he left the restroom. Anthony exited right being him with a smirk on his face.

"I'll see you later. I gotta go," Josh explained. Josh looked down the hallways and then sprinted out the building.

Anthony stood in front of the restroom for a couple seconds. He wanted to go back inside. He had found what he had been looking for his whole life. His phone rang.

Persela: Hey baby bae.

Anthony: *I'm a bit busy. ttyl*

The class had already begun when Anthony walked in. Luckily, no one noticed him as he entered and calmly sat into an empty seat near the back where he hoped no one would acknowledge him. Sitting down, a girl looked over.

"Oh, my God, are you ok?" she asked, "There's blood on your knuckles."

"Yea, I'm fine," Anthony said shoving her off. He looked around and wondered if anyone heard her comment. Luckily, everyone was busy working on their paper. Anthony tried wiping the blood off with his shirt.

"Seriously," the young girl said deeply disturbed in Anthony. "That's disgusting." She turned to the professor's direction and stood up. She was ready to open her mouth when Anthony reached over and pulled her back to her seat.

"Shut the fuck up, it's not that serious," Anthony said releasing her and getting up from his seat. Walking out the classroom, his phone rang.

"Babe, are you ok? Everyone's saying you're covered in blood and limping. Is it true?" Persela asked.

"I'm fine," Anthony replied surprised at how fast rumors escalated. *Limping, people must be confusing me with Marc,* he thought.

"I'm leaving class right now and headed to you. Leave the door unlocked," Persela said.

114

"Stop, Persela, I don't need anyone coming over. I'm fine. I just need some time alone," Anthony said but it was too late. Persela had already hung up. "Goddamnit, Persela. I shouldn't have fucking picked up. That's what you get, Anthony." He thought about calling her back but couldn't think of what to say.

Persela and Helene walked in moments after Anthony. Anthony sighed just seeing Persela's worried face. Her eyes quickly began to well with tears seeing a shirt on his floor with a blood stain on it. She bolted toward Anthony, who was laying on his bed, and jumped on him. Wrapping her arms around him, she started crying. Helene sat at the edge of his bed looking down at the floor not saying a word. Persela grabbed his arm and inspected it. She reached over his face and ran her fingers through his hair and the back of his neck.

"I don't see anything," she said.

"Like I said, I'm fine," Anthony responded.

"The blood. Whose blood is that?" Persela said no longer crying.

"It's," he started then stopped to think what he was going to say. "It's a long story. A story I don't feel like telling," Anthony finished. He rubbed his face and turned away from her. "Anyways, shouldn't you be in class or something," he asked Persela.

"No, I'm gonna stay here and keep you company. You had me worried. Besides I'm already here," Persela suggested in her bubbly attitude. She jumped closer to him.

"Fuck off, Persela," Anthony finally said. Persela jerked back and froze. It was the first time Anthony had ever said something like that to her. She wanted to say something that would calm him or do something that would please him, but she was too shocked to think.

"Ok, I'll come back later. Text me when you feel any better," Persela said faintly. Helene followed.

Walking out the room, Persela shyly looked over at Helene expecting her to explain what had just happened. If anyone, besides

Josh, knew Anthony it was her. She tried getting a response but Helene wasn't entirely there. She hated how Helene was always high on something.

"Man, that kid got his ass kicked," Helene finally spoke. Persela waited for Helene to explain but Helene seemed to have forgotten the conversation she had just started as her attention was turned to the clouds in the sky. She reached up as if she could reach out to touch them.

"What are you talking about, Helene?" Persela asked not able shove the subject away.

"What?" Helene said.

"Who was it?" Persela tried asking another question.

"Who?"

———

For the first time, Josh was scared. He was in his final year of college, and there was now the possibility that he might not graduate. He needed leverage. He needed Ben. After the fight with Marc, Josh quickly left and began searching for him. He was the only one who could help him cover the whole incident as if it never happened. He had that kind of power. All Josh had to do was find him, but with no social network, phone number, or any way of finding him, all he could do was hope he crossed paths with him. Sadly, after a long search Ben was nowhere to be seen. As the day ended and not hearing anything about the incident, he figured he was safe for the night. He would continue his search tomorrow.

"Josh," a voice calmly called out from behind. Josh stopped and turned, for the first time he was happy to hear Ben's voice.

Ben was not the most attractive person Josh knew. At first glance, he seemed slow. He had the body of a giant. He was tall with a square face. His cheeks were always blushing pink. He had a large nose that seemed more birdlike than human. He never smiled but had a calm face. And just like his face, he walked undisturbed. Taking every

116

step with no rush. Josh always wondered if his walking had anything to do with the slight hunch on his back.

"I heard everything," Ben said sighing with his deep and slow tone.

"I lost my cool and," Josh started explaining. "well, me and Anthony lost our cool."

"Well, this kid hasn't contacted anyone, and I don't think he's going to," explained Ben.

"What do you mean?" Josh asked confused.

"He left campus right after it happened. He did though report to all his professors that he was feeling ill and wouldn't be attending class for a couple days."

"The kid's not stupid," Josh said.

"He isn't, but you are. Anyways, I'm sorry I couldn't see you earlier. But next time some kid upsets you or any of your friends, let me handle it," Ben suggested as he gave Josh a piercing look. "Let this be the last time something like this happens. Remember you have a responsibility. I need you in the University keeping an eye on things. If you can't handle the job. I will gladly replace you." Josh looked away as Ben was the only person he truly feared.

"Sorry, Ben," Josh said lowering his head.

"Oh, before I forget, bring Anthony to the house tomorrow," Ben said. Trying not to say much, Josh simply nodded. "First thing in the morning, I've arranged everything with his and your professors. Doctor's appointment," Ben said. Josh nodded again.

"All right," Josh said respectfully.

"Good night, Joshua," Ben said walking away.

———

That night, Anthony and Josh met Persela and Helene outside the hookah lounge. Waiting in line, her eyes wandered into the city

117

scenery as she listened to the hip-hop music that echoed from inside. Persela couldn't help but feel as if she was expecting to see someone. She looked across the street at a bar that was lit with lights and music. She reached over to grab Anthony's hand.

"You have my I.D. right babe?" Helene asked.

"Why would I have your I.D.?" Josh snapped.

"Well I don't have it, check your pocket," Helene demanded. Josh searched his pockets.

"Persela, I thought you had her I.D." Josh stated.

"No," Persela said as she caught sight of a man walking out of a bar with a cigar in his mouth. Persela had a strange feeling that she had been in a situation like this before.

"Never mind. I have it!" Helene announced as they approached the bouncer.

"Oh, let's sit there," Helene said walking in. They sat down and ordered a mango-flavored hookah.

"I'm ready to graduate," Helene said pulling out a pack of cigarettes. She lit the cigarette and placed it between her lips. She handed the pack to Persela, who lit one as well.

Persela looked out the window at the stranger smoking the cigar. "I wanna dance!" Persela giggled and got up. She grabbed Anthony, who looked at her confused. She knew he wasn't the dancing type but couldn't help the urge to dance with him. He did not budge from his seat. Before feeling embarrassed, or worse, embarrassing him, she turned around and sat on his lap and began giving him a lap dance until the hookah was brought to them.

"I wanna go see this new movie that's coming out. We should all go!" Persela said. She waited for Anthony to say something. He looked occupied inside his own mind. *What wrong with him?* she wondered. She began to feel self-conscious. *Is it the way I dressed or did I say something?*

118

"Yea, we should all go. What do you think, Josh?" Helene said looking at Josh. He was inhaling the tobacco. "What movie is it?"

"Ummmm," Persela bit her lower lip. "Baby, help me. It's with that actor we both like. He's in those action movies." Anthony didn't respond. He grabbed the hookah pipe and ignored Persela's question. "Oh, my God, it's gonna bother me all night."

"We should go check out this new club that opened," Josh suggested.

"Yea, baby, we should go. Maybe after this!" Helene said. She looked at Persela and Anthony.

"Yea." She looked at Anthony, who was handing the pipe to her. Grabbing the pipe, Anthony exhaled the fumes above his head.

"I'm not really feeling it tonight you guys," Anthony said. Getting up, he walked out without saying another word.

Persela and Helene followed behind him. When they stepped out, Anthony was already on the other side of the street.

"Sometimes I feel like he doesn't even love me."

"He does Persela." Helene argued. "I know he does. Just the way he looks at you. Sometimes I even get jealous 'cause Josh doesn't even look at me like that, you know?"

"You think so? You really think so?" Persela could not envision Anthony's love. She wondered what Helene saw that she could not. "You really think so?"

"Yea. Trust me. I wish I could get Josh to look at me the way Anthony does to you."

"I think I'm done for the night Helene. You and Josh have fun." Persela said still trying to figure out the kind of love Anthony had for her. Feeling abandoned, she bit her lower lip. *What is going on with Anthony?* she thought. She stood on the curb thinking if she had done something to have upset him.

"He's a fuckin' asshole. Isn't he?" asked a shadow from the street. Persela jumped by the stranger's comment. It was Marc. He had his hands in his pockets as a cigarette rested on his ear. His long uncombed hair covered his black eye. Persela looked up at him then down at her feet. "You know out of all the people I know there's something about you," Marc started. Persela looked up somewhat offended. "Not in a bad way. I mean, maybe. I don't know. It's like I hate the feeling because I don't understand it."

"What?" Persela asked trying to understand what he was trying to say. Without knowing, they smiled at each other's confusion.

"God, I wanna know everything that makes you smile."

"Anyways, so what are you doing out?" Persela asked giggling.

"I live right there," Marc said pointing at a building while reaching for his cigarette. He placed it on his lip but didn't light it. "For someone who believes everyone should be happy, you don't' seem so happy." Persela looked up at him. She looked back down trying to hide a tear that had escaped her eye. "You really believe that everyone should be happy and all that?"

"Yea," Persela shrugged her shoulders.

"I don't," Marc said. Persela looked up completely forgetting about Anthony abandoning her. "I don't want to call it sadness or pain. I don't know what to call it but whatever it is, inspires me."

"Inspires what?"

"I'm an artist," Marc declared.

"Wow, really, what kind of artist?" Persela asked curiously. "You don't really come off as the artist kind of person."

"Yea, I know. I kinda get that a lot."

"You come off as more of a… I don't know. Maybe a. I don't know what you come off as but an artist isn't one."

"Yea, well, I am."

"I don't' believe you. Where's your studio."

"Come on. I'll show you," he stretched his hand out and tightly held on to Persela's hand. A jolt of excitement ran through Persela's body as they dodged incoming cars. She giggled as someone honked their horn. Marc's spontaneous attitude brought Persela energy back. They entered the rusted old building and made their way to the second floor.

"You ever played knock knock ditch," Marc asked.

"Yea when I was a kid," Persela answered.

"Well I hope your fast," Marc said as he went to the first door and furiously knocked on it. Persela jolted down the hallway. Marc followers behind her. She was ready to turn down another hallway when Marc grabbed her by the hand. "Wrong way! Wrong way! This way!"

"Oh, my god!" Persela said giggling.

"Damn fuckin' kids. I'm find you!" Someone yelled as they ran up the stairs.

"Shhhhh," Marc suggested then laughing.

"Ok. Ok." Persela said with a childish smile on her face. Marc led her to apartment 205. Inside, curtains hung from the ceiling to the floor on every wall. A small window was cracked open where she could look at the street below. It had a small balcony, large enough for one person.

"Sorry, I hate the red brick. I hope you don't mind the curtains dancing all over the place."

"No, I love it!" Persela shouted. "Oh, you are an artist! Like an actual artist." She noticed an empty canvas sitting on a tripod in one of the rooms in front of a bed covered with white sheets. She walked inside and noticed more paintings in every size with all sorts of colors, some realistic and some abstract. She was speechless inside his studio. "Your artwork is amazing. I've actually seen some of these in the school's gallery," she said running her fingers through countless

121

canvases. "So, you're Marc? Like that – Marc. The artist Marc. I don't know why I never put two and two together."

"In the flash," Marc said bowing down. He smiled then reached into his pocket for a lighter.

"Paint me," Persela said stepping towards him then shyly taking a step back. She locked eyes with him. He lost his balance and dropped his lighter.

"What?" he stuttered with disbelief. It was all so sudden and quick. He had not imagined his night to have ended this way.

"I want you to paint me!" Persela demanded more confidently. "Or, am I not good enough to be your muse?"

"I can't. It doesn't really work that way," Marc said firmly. Picking up his lighter he placed it back in his pocket.

"Why not?" Persela felt offended. Marc made his way to Persela. He stood in front of her. He looked down at her feet and began studying every inch of her body. "Why not?" she asked gently. As his eyes wondered about her body, her legs grew weary. She bit her lower lip not knowing what was about to happen.

"I have to study your body. Every inch of it. Every curve. I need to explore it."

"Yea," Persela whispered. Marc pressed his lips up against hers, then picked her up from her feet and carried her to the bed, knocking over his tripod on the way. Jumping on the bed, he pulled the covers over them. Marc pulled away to look at her glimmering eyes, he kissed her lips then made his way to her neck where he gently bit her. He stopped. Persela looked up at the sheets over her face, she closed her eyes. She could feel his lips hovering above her breast and stomach. His long hair tickled her skin. Marc reached over and grabbed her hand. He held it tightly as he raised it above her. His other hand calmly landed on her waist, where it started exploring every part of her. It found tickle spots she did not know about. *What is he doing?* Persela thought as Marc took his time appreciating every curve. Persela moaned. She had never been adored or touched so passionately in her life. She felt like a piece of artwork being sculpted by his hands. Marc's hands moved to unbutton her pants when Anthony crossed her mind, Persela wanted to push him away but could not. No one in her life had ever touched her this way and probably never would. Before she realized it, her pants were off. Marc kissed her left knee. He gently made his way down her thigh and to her stomach. His hands stretched out towards hers.

"Your body is a wonderland," Marc whispered. He came back up to look at Persela. "You're a piece of art, Persela."

"Yea," Persela moaned. Marc kissed her collar bone as Persela pulled his pants down. He quickly took off his shirt. That's when she noticed his black eye. "What happened?"

"Fell down some stairs," Marc replied as he reached over and pulled her shirt off.

Persela had never felt so loved in her life. Marc held her tightly in his arms. She could not help but hold him back and never wanting to let go. She kissed him afraid of losing the moment to time. Their tongues explored one another. He bit her lower lip. One of his hands reached behind her neck and pushed her closer towards him. She reached her hand over his neck and did the same. Letting go of her neck, he reached over and gripped her thigh.

She reached over and laid her head on his chest when they finished. She placed her hand on his stomach. They found themselves in complete silence. Nothing needed to be said as they quickly felt a sense of comfort with one another. Persela had never been comfortably quiet with someone before. Persela looked up and stared into his eyes, they were completely oblivious to everything around them. Marc looked over at her and could not help but admire her eyes.

"You have the prettiest eyes," he whispered.

"No, I don't," she said giggling. She turned over and hid under the blanket. Chasing after her, she screeched, "No, stop! I'm ticklish."

He stopped the moment her eyes caught his. Concealed from the world, they felt alone. And for the first time, Persela didn't mind.

"No, seriously. I've never seen eyes like that," Marc explained. "I've always loved the color brown."

"They're just eyes."

"They're your eyes though."

"I love your painting," Persela said.

"They're just paintings."

"What made you want to paint?"

"My mother. She was a painter."

"She must be proud of you. So, is painting like a family thing?"

"I hope and not really. But the smell of oil reminds me of her."

Chapter XIV

"So, where the hoes at?" Anthony shouted in excitement. He reached under his feet and grabbed a beer.

"Chill, what about Persela? I can't believe you left her," Casey said in disbelief.

"Yea, really. I can't believe you left me with Helene by myself." Josh said. Everyone laughed. "You my friend are a fuckin' dick."

"Ha ha, fuck that. I can't believe you left Helene! Remember that one time we put that one bitch in the trunk," Anthony said.

"Yes, oh shit! I complete forgotten about that," Daniel laughed.

"Yea and we forget about her till next morning!" Casey yelled hysterically. Everyone stopped to think trying to remember if they had just put anyone in the trunk that night. No one could remember.

"Oh shit!" they all yelled. Justin pulled over, they all ran to the trunk to check if anyone was in there. Empty. Relieved, they jumped back into the car and sped down the freeway.

"Look, Casey, I'ma be completely honest with you alright," Anthony quickly glanced over at Daniel and Josh.

"60," Daniel shouted.

"Let's do this shit!" Josh shouted.

"I don't care if you get back with Jen. I really don't, and I'm saying this because I know in the back of every man's mind he's always thinking what his boys are thinking. 'Oh, I don't want my friends to think I'm a pussy.' That's not it."

"Nah, Nah. Yea. I feel you."

"Man, if she makes you happy, go for it, you know. I just want you to know that I love you. Whatever makes you happy. I just want you to make sure that you know that I don't care. That no one cares really," Anthony stopped to take a sip of his beer.

"Yea, it just ain't the same, you know," Casey started.

"Yea."

"She left me. And she knows she fucked up. She knows."

"90," Josh shouted. Street lights began passing by them like rays of light.

"I could never take her back. I mean we're still hanging out and shit. I told her, 'Hey we can chill, fuck, whatever, but don't expect anything.'"

"Yea?" Anthony said.

"But."

"But were getting old for this dating shit, ain't we?" Anthony finished.

"Exactly," Casey admitted. "What do I care? Like, you think I wanna go back to texting bitches good morning and good night? Then asking them when their birthday is. And what their favorite color is? Fuck that!"

"I don't give a fuck what your favorite color is, bitch. This is gonna sound horrible, but I don't know Persela's favorite color and I really don't give a shit." Anthony and Casey laughed.

"It's just a lot of work. Take 'em out for dinner a movie. Get to know 'em. Fuck that," Casey reached over Anthony's leg and also grabbed a beer.

"130," Daniel shouted.

"Come on motherfucker!" Josh shouted. "I wanna die t'night."

Casey opened his beer. "So, I don't know if I really wanna get back with her. Like I do but just knowing that someone else had been inside her fucks it all up. But I don't wanna go back out to the dating scene. Know what I mean?"

"Yea."

"160," shouted Josh and Daniel.

"160 miles per hour motherfuckers!" Josh shouted, beating on the dashboard, and shaking his dreadlocks everywhere. Daniel did the same. Casey and Anthony beat on the headliner. They screamed in excitement like wild beasts until Anthony noticed they missed their exit.

"Yo, yo, yo! Goddamnit, you missed the exit."

Daniel slowed the car down. Everyone's energy slowly faded. Without warning, Daniel pulled to the left and made a U-turn on the median. He was ready to pull into the exit when red and blue lights flashed behind them. Everyone panicked.

"Oh shit. What the fuck do I do with this? We're fucked," Josh said digging through his pockets. Anthony reached over, grabbing the bag of weed from Josh, and swallowed it whole.

"Problem fixed," he said with a mouthful. "You got anything else?" Anthony said with a grin on his face.

"The beer," Casey said. They were all empty, but before they could completely hide them under their seats, the cop was already on Daniel's window. Daniel froze. The officer tapped on the window. He rolled it down.

"Can you please get out of the vehicle?" Daniel thought about running but every time he reached over for the keys he panicked and brought his hand back. Slowly reaching for the door handle, he stepped out. Two empty beer bottles fell out with him.

"We're fucked," Casey whispered.

"He's fucked," Anthony whispered under his breath.

Daniel looked up at the officer with a face of defeat. "Look, Officer, I just wanna go home. I didn't' get no pussy tonight so it's been a shitty night. I just wanna go home. It's just the next exit. Come on, cut me some slack."

The officer gave a small but noticeable smirk and without saying another word walked back to his patrol car. Daniel watched the officer drive off before getting back in his car.

———

"I hope you seriously didn't just take me behind the university to take me on a jog bro," Anthony said.

"No. Not at all. Anyways, I can't believe that motherfucker cop let us go last night. I really thought we were all going to jail," Josh said. Kicking a pebble towards the street, he looked up as if looking for something. "So, where'd you end up going after we dropped you off?"

"Tatyana," Anthony said with a smirk.

"Damn, really, Persela hasn't found out. No scratch that. Tatyana hasn't found out?" Josh asked concerned.

"Nah, fuck that. So, how's you and Helene?"

"Horrible, fuckin' horrible," Josh said looking down. "It's like she doesn't see what's she's doing with herself. I'm not complaining, but we're not kids anymore. I wanna help her, but I don't know how." Anthony tried listening to everything Josh had to say but was already irritated by having been woken up earlier than usual. "Anyways we broke up," Josh finished. Stunned, Anthony was ready to ask him what exactly happened when he was cut off. "We're here."

Out there, in the middle of nowhere, a two-story red brick house stood before them. It looked like any other house but seemed out of place as if a storm had picked it up and dropped it off in the woods. Walking closer to the house, Anthony looked up at an attic window. He noticed the infinity sign engraved inside the circular shaped window. Josh knocked on the door. The door opened slowly to reveal Ben standing inside.

"You're late," Ben said calmly. "Work on your timing. I have other things to do than wait for people."

"I'm sorry, Ben, I'm just," Josh started but was quickly cut off.

"Keep your girlfriend problems away when it comes to The Pool Table Club," Ben said as Josh's face reddened. Anthony's eyes widened. He imagined Josh losing control and pounding on the tall, bird-like man.

"I'm sorry. Anyway, I have to go." Josh said turning away.

"A disappointment." Ben stared at Josh like a hawk as he made his way back. "So, you're Anthony?" Ben asked. His eyes still glued on Josh. "Come in, Tony."

Inside, the house was empty. Anthony had expected seeing furniture, electronic appliances, and club members. Instead, the entire place looked deserted, no television, no couches, no table, or club members. He looked into the kitchen, also empty. It had no refrigerator or oven. If it weren't for the sink, Anthony would not have guessed it was a kitchen. Confused he turned to Ben for an explanation.

"Follow me," Ben said walking up the steps. Anthony followed him up the steps and through a hallway of empty bedrooms. At the end of the hallway, Ben reached up to a piece of rope from the ceiling. Pulling it down, a set of stairs unfolded. The attic was large and unlike the other rooms, it had three bunk beds in the far back, a stove, and a refrigerator. Ben walked over to the window and glared at everything around him.

"The Pool Table Club," Ben started. "It's more than what people think," Anthony walked towards Ben. He waited for whatever Ben was getting ready to tell him. "The Pool Table Club, Division Campus, is in charge of the organization. We make sure that everything gets sorted and accounted for," Anthony wondered what he was referring to. "Do you understand Tony," Ben turned to Anthony then looked at his wrist watch. "They're here." Anthony looked outside and saw a line of white vans driving through the woods. They pulled up in a line, six men stepped out the first van. Three of the men walked inside the house as the other three began hauling duffle bags inside. It took them no longer than two minutes before all six returned and drove off. The next van pulled up next and did the same.

"What's in the duffle bags?" Ben didn't respond. He just looked down at them, counting every duffle bag that entered his house. A total of ten vans passed.

"Ten, we expected less," Ben said. He walked away and approached the staircase.

"Come on, Tony."

Downstairs, the entire house was filled with duffle bags. Ben, freely walked on top of them, not caring if he damaged whatever was inside. Unlike Anthony, who tried his best to step lightly as he followed Ben into the kitchen. Ben opened a duffle bag. He grabbed what was inside and tossed it to Anthony. It hit his chest and bounced off. He caught it in time before it fell on the floor. Anthony's eyes widened in shock at what he was holding. A band of hundred-dollar bills. He could not help but place his thumb on the edge and flip through all the bills. Ten-thousand dollars tossed like it was worthless.

"The Pool Table Club is more than a club for campus students. It is a business," Ben explained. "A very important business."

"Like drugs," Anthony said trying to sound familiar with what the club was involved in but instead Ben scowled Anthony, suggesting that be the last time he cut him off.

"Like drugs, loans, exotic vacation, a nice ring, anything, Tony. Drugs is the tip of the iceberg. Drugs is just a way to make money. What you do with that money, is what really counts. This brings me to what I brought you here. Because we are students of an institution, we are the more suitable candidates for managing something so grand. Do you understand, Tony?" asked Ben as he walked towards Anthony. Anthony nodded, handing back the band of money to Ben. Ben reached out his hand and pushed the money back. "It's yours. In the Pool Table Club, we have a hazing tradition I enjoy," Ben began explaining. Anthony gulped as imagines rendered in his mind of what was about to happen. That's when Ben spoke, "what can I do, Anthony, to make your dreams became a reality?"

"Wha- What?" Anthony asked confused. Anthony was unprepared. He had no idea what to say and Ben staring straight at him only made him feel more pressured. "I want to be great. I want power," Anthony said honestly but became embarrassed having told someone, who he barely knew, his inner thoughts and dreams.

"Hmmm," Ben simply said looking at Anthony. "What if I offered you all this, everything? What if I said you can have it all? You can have my power and position in The Pool Table Club. Would that be good enough?"

Anthony imagined being in Ben's position. An enormous smile grew on his face. He tried restraining it, but it was hard after being told he could have what he's always dreamed of, power.

"Yea," Anthony said smiling like a child. "And what about you?" Anthony asked. Ben smiled for the first time.

"First, I have to teach you a couple of things and show you how everything works," Ben explained. "The Pool Table Club works like a clock and like any clock, it depends on the smallest gears to do their part so that the bigger gears turn properly. It takes the smallest of people and actions that allow the bigger and greater things in life to become a possibility," Ben waved his hands in the air trying to illustrate the mechanics of a clock. "The Pool Table Club has three divisions in whatever city it is occupying, and it's necessary that all three exist for the system to work."

"So, who are the rest of the club members. The two other divisions."

"Tony, there are things even I have no knowledge of. When I was introduced to the club, I was given little information. Enough to keep the organization going and make it a success. Anyways, being a college students we practice business, political system, and military tactics in classrooms but also in The Pool Table Club."

"How?"

"Simple, students studying business helps us maintain the club financially. Members practicing political science occupy organizations around school campus and help elect certain students into certain offices as well as other political tactics," Ben smiled greatly at his accomplishment. "I'm aware this is no army, but we do practice military tactics. This is a somewhat dangerous business, but when others want to start their own little business, we take them down with little to no force. No small force can be given the slightest of opportunity. I know I am not making much sense. I will try to explain as much as I can later. Back to what I was saying. There is more to The Pool Table Club inside, but all you need to know is what's going on in campus. We do deal with narcotics. But like I said. We are more fit for this. Do you understand, Tony?" Ben asked and without waiting for an answer he continued. "Our goal is not to induce students into a life of crime and corruption. Our intention is to give students a stronger understanding of their practice and continue to keep a strong tie with The Pool Table Club. And since the beginning of the club, The Pool Table Club now has members in political parties, large corporate businesses, as well as military officials overseas. We are a worldwide force."

132

It was nearly impossible for Anthony to keep up with everything Ben was telling him. It was more than what he had imagined. He remembered the conversation he had with Josh. Everything Josh had told him was true, only now it was different. Josh was speculating out of rumors and here was Ben telling him that all the rumors were true.

"I thought these were only rumors?" asked Anthony.

"Josh only told you so much." Ben once again looked down at his watch. "Timing is important and vital. They should be here any time now."

"Who's in charge of everything? Whose above all this? Above you?" Anthony asked.

"God," Ben said without hesitation. The door swung open, a group of people stormed inside and grabbing a duffle bag, sprinting to the attic. "Let's step outside, shall we?" Ben suggested.

"I want you to report after all your classes back here. I have more to tell you. People you have to meet and other things. You're majoring in business so it will all sound familiar, but I need you to understand in detail what makes everything work and why. I will say something that I need you to know. Like I said to Josh, I will say the same to you. I don't care how you do it, but your girl, family, and any kind of problems stay far away from the club. Do you understand, Tony? I don't and you don't need any kind of distractions." Ben looked down at his watch again.

"Yea," was all Anthony could say.

"Good. I'll see you Monday," Ben walked back into the brick house. It sounded like a madhouse as everyone inside yelled numbers into the air.

Anthony made his way back to campus and outside the fence. He looked back at the school trying to fathom that deep within the blood red brick wall that surrounded Sapien University, The Pool Table Club resided. A club that did not exist but only in myths and

133

legends. He felt honored, as only a selected few were handpicked to join the club. An organization that ran drug trafficking, extortion, money laundering, and obstruction of justice. He felt like a gangster from a movie. It was everything Anthony dreamed of and more. It was a society that seized your wildest dreams and presented them to reality, where lies became truth, and the separation from reality and fantasy were finally brought down. And as for the engineer or engineers behind such grandiose institution, no one knew. Not even those inside the club. It did not matter, Anthony was going to seize power and overlook down on everyone very soon. He was going to become God.

Chapter XV

October 3, 2011
Love at first sight

Tapping on the table, I tried my best to ignore the clock's ticking noise. I looked around the new library, then across to some empty seats. I got up and glanced through the bookshelves, nothing looked interesting. Giving up, I sat back down and listened to a group of students complain about the research they had been assigned. Sitting across from me, they opened their book and grunted in agony. I couldn't help but think back to my days in high school and the love I had for reading and writing. Now that I thought about it, it had been a while since I'd written anything. I thought about writing Mrs. Deborah's letter but decided not to. Instead, I got up and once again lost myself within the aisles of bookshelves.

***

Mrs. Deborah was one of those teachers that came to the nearest library to help kids with school work, kind of like an after-school program. One day, I picked up a book one of her student neglected. She noticed and from then on, she kept her eye on me until I finished it. I don't remember what the title was, who wrote it, or what it was about but from the first word to the last, I read it with ease. I never bothered checking it out. Bending the top corner, of whatever page I was on, I'd leave it on the table. The next day it would be right there where I left it. While everyone was barely in the first couple chapters, I was already half through mine. Maybe because I wasn't a student. I never stopped to take notes or ponder on what the writer might have meant. I was lucky enough to enjoy the book, the way a piece of literature should be read.

"What did you think of the book?" Mrs. Deborah asked me one day.

"It was ok," I replied trying to walk away.

"So where do you go to school?"

"I don't," I was ready to say something but changed my mind.

"Have you started applying for scholarships? What colleges are you interested in going?" She was persistent and difficult to ignore. So, I decided to amuse myself and pretend I was a high school student and that my life was as normal as anyone else's.

For the next month, we grew a strong teacher student relationship, she would tease me about my slow reading and before finishing a book, she would already have a pile of books for me to read. Before I knew it, I had assignments and due dates. I had to write a summary and give honest opinions on whatever book she recommended. I couldn't resist doing them. It felt good being a student again. There were times I would put my job on the line and stay up late, just because I felt that a sentence wasn't written the right way. Every other night I would have to remind myself that I wasn't a high school student. Sometimes I thought about telling her the truth but never did. I felt proud whenever she would snatch my paper out of my hands and scrambled through the words. "Who wrote this? Cause I know you didn't," she would joke.

I was turning in my latest assignment when Mrs. Deborah asked me, "What do you think about those that lie to themselves." My mind was already racing with ideas. "Have you started looking into scholarships? You get my email with the one about Spanish speakers." I didn't say anything. I just nodded my head. "Well, you better get on it. Your future isn't gonna wait on you."

I felt horrible. My lie had gone on too far and now I couldn't continue with it. I had run out of excuses as to why I hadn't applied for scholarships or picked a college. For the first time in my life, I had done wrong to someone who had done nothing but help me.

I never went back to that library. Embarrassed and ashamed, I couldn't bring myself to look Mrs. Deborah in the face and tell her the truth. The whole situation bothered me. Sometimes I would think about going back and coming clean with her, but I never did build up the courage. That's when I thought about writing her a letter and explaining the situation and apologizing at the same time. I wrote about twenty letters, but not one came out the way I wanted it to. A simple sorry wasn't enough. Day in and day out, my mind raced with words and phrases. Even at work, I couldn't get my mind to focus. I thought about taking a day off but never did. And it wasn't until my accident that it was too late.

***

"Pick any book. They are all relevant." A told myself. "Relevant to what?" *Mrs. Deborah would have already picked out a book for me*, I thought. "Life," I said to no one. I got up and walked down the rows of bookshelves. I finally reached over and grabbed a book. Looking through the pages, nothing popped out to me. I placed it back, grabbing the next book I did the same. On to the next row. I picked another random book and once again scanned through the pages. Nothing interesting. Ready to place it back, something finally grabbed my attention. Looking through the slot where the book belonged, I saw someone.

She had caramel like skin that looked smooth as silk. Her natural curled hair came down to her lower back. Her eyes glimmered as she focused down at a picture puzzle she was doing. Blinking, her eyelashes flapped like butterfly wings. She bit her lower lip in frustration and using her fingers, she combed her hair back. I thought about approaching her but decided not to. I placed the book back in its place, removing the view.

137

Returning to my seat, I began regretting coming. I looked down at my bandaged hands. I felt stupid. As if I could even hold a book right now, I thought.

"I don't think you're gonna be doing any reading," a girl spoke. I looked up. It was the same girl I had been spying on. "You want to help me separate some picture puzzles. They got mixed up in the same box." I didn't know what to say.

"Ummm, yeah, sure," I said.

We scrambled through the pieces, trying hard to separate the right pieces into the right group. I glanced at her. She was focused. I wanted to say something, but nothing came to mind. Having nothing to say I helped her unscramble the puzzles in silence.

We separated the puzzles but two pieces that were joined together. They fit perfectly together but came from two separate images.

"Let me see," she said giggling. She held them and tried twisting them apart. They twisted together and did not separate. "Weird huh?"

"Let's leave 'em," I suggested not wanting to separate the two.

"No, there not meant for each other." She forcefully broke their bond and placed them inside their proper boxes. "So, what happened to your hands?" she asked looking down at them.

"Fire torch accident at my job," I said. She made a painful facial expression.

"Did it hurt?"

"It actually didn't. Well, I didn't feel it."

"What do you mean?"

"It happened so fast, I don't really remember. It's one of those things that before you know it, it's over."

"So, what kind of work do you do? Sorry my name's Ovella, what's yours?" she reached her hand out. "Oh, my God. I'm so sorry."

"It's fine."

"So how does that machine work? Is it hard? Has anyone died doing that? I would never do that. I don't think anyone would." Ovella asked me question after question and just as I was ready to learn about her she looked at her phone and explained she was late for a school meeting.

"It was nice meeting you," I said.

"Same time tomorrow," she said smiling.

The next day, everything seemed colorful and brighter. Nothing was as dark as it used to be. I couldn't help but smile when I saw her waiting outside the library. "How are your hands," she asked. "I hope you don't mind sitting with some friends from school."

"It's fine." If her friends were anything like she was, I didn't mind. Two guys sat reading a book. They had tight jeans, band shirts, long beards, large glasses, and one of them had a nose ring and a sleeve tattoo. A girl was taking down notes. I was introduced, but they didn't seem to care. They continued their reading. Ovella handed a book over to the one with a nose ring. "Read the highlighted parts and tell me what you think."

"Me and Ricky were talking the other day. And he said something that just made me think."

"What he say, Jasmine?" Ovella asked curious to know.

"Trees, why do we call them that. What if that's not what they want to be called." Jasmine stopped. "That's when I realized, why do we identify each other as black, white, or whatever? You know what I mean?" Everyone stopped what they were doing to look and her and think about what she had just said.

"It's society, man," stated Jack. I could not help but stop reading. I looked up, being reminded of Oreo and his long night rants.

"Revolution, people need to start waking up. They need to wake up from this fake lifestyle. It's separating and killing us. That's all its doing. From the beginning, they've been trying to separate us. Divide us." explained Corey. I looked over his sleeve tattoo and nose piercing. They all nodded in agreement then turned to look at me. I gave a light chuckle. I couldn't believe what I was hearing.

"What's so funny? I don't see the funny side of a corrupt government or the deaths of millions going to pointless wars."

"Yea man. How about you get educated and read a book on the world you're living in?"

"Jackass."

I couldn't help but be bothered by their remarks. "I'ma be honest with yah. What yah consider political issues, I don't."

"What? Are you listening to yourself?" someone said.

"Corrupt government, pointless wars, hate, chaos, all that stuff. That's life. First off, I wasn't born here. I came from a place where by the time you were twelve you knew how to hold a gun. By the time you were twelve, you've lost half your friends. And I didn't cry because it's normal. And there isn't a funeral because their family can't afford a proper burial ground. And no matter how many die. The violence never stops because…" I was saying too much, but I couldn't stop. "And the most horrible thing of it all is that no one knows they're suffering because they've never felt joy before." With that, I had nothing more to say. I looked over at Ovella, and before my face could turn red, I got up and left. How much had I said about myself? I didn't know, and I didn't want to find out. Everything started turning back as it once was, dark and dull.

"Alejandro!" I couldn't help but stop and turn around whenever she called my name.

"I'm so sorry," was all I could say.

"For what? I mean, it's fine. I mean Corey is quite the dick sometimes." Ovella said smiling. "Maybe we should hang out just the two of us. I live down the street. The blue house with a swing. I know. How corny is that?"

We made our way outside the library. Nothing was said. I was still afraid that I would reveal my dark past to someone I had just met. I looked over at her and wondered if she was thinking about what I had said earlier. I wanted to tell her that none of it was true and somehow show her I was just a normal teenage boy but I didn't know how to.

Stepping inside the large blue house, a large man was sitting in the living room watching TV. He was brown skinned and well built. He didn't say anything, and neither did I. He kept a close eye on me as we walked over to the dining table where piles of papers laid scattered everywhere.

"How's your hands?" Ovella asked again.

"They're ok. How's school work?" I asked glancing over at the large man.

"I wish I had torched hands," Ovella said pouting. "I'd look like such a badass. No one would dare step up to me," she tried giving a threatening look. I couldn't help but laugh. "I'm being serious," I quickly stopped. Her eyes lit up as she laughed.

"No, you don't." Trying to change the topic I asked, "so what exactly are you doin'?"

"I'm studying for my final exams."

"And who is this," said a woman. An exceptionally tall woman with braided hair and dark skin stood on the front door. I waited for her to say something as she continued to look at me with a large smile on her face. But after a long awkward silence, she glanced at her husband. He got up, and they both disappeared behind a door.

"So, when did the doctor say he's going to take the bandages off?"

"Doctor? I didn't see one," I replied. "Rocky poured some alcohol on it and bandaged it up with my shirt." Her face was starting to look concerned. Appalled that I did not seek medical attention and at how I was not bothered by it. "I took them off last night. It's healed but," I looked down at my hands. "I don't want you to see them. Anyways so what's your favorite color?"

"No! Not fair. You can't just change the topic like that!"

"I just feel like you know more about me than I do about you."

"Yea, you're right," Ovella said pouting. I loved the way she pouted. "It's purple. I'm pretty tired of studying," she said getting off the dinner table and walking over to the living room.

We watched television on the same couch without saying a word. I wanted to say something but what? I tried to think of something to say so that she knew I was interested in her but nothing crossed my mind. I glanced at her. She looked focused on the television screen. I was beginning to have my doubts and wondered what I was doing there. My mind was racing with excuses as I thought about leaving.

"I like you," she said. I bit my lip trying to hold back an enormous smile. "You don't say much. But I can tell you have a lot to say. There's more to you and I can tell. You're not like everyone else. Your interesting." She stopped looking me up and down as if trying got figure me out with a single glance. "You never smile or frown. Like you're always thinking."

She moved over and grabbed my hand. I jerked it back. "I'm sorry," I said.

"No!" She jumped on top and restrained me from going anywhere. "Let me see your hands. Let's see your cool battle scar!" Quickly, without giving me a chance to react, she removed the bandage covering my hands. Embarrassed at how rough my hands were, I tried closing my palms but feeling her gentle hands I couldn't help but let her fingers swirl around mine. She moved up towards my knuckles, where my scars were. She didn't gasp in horror the way I imagined her doing. She looked up at me with a gentle smile and wrapped her arms around me. "I think your scars are pretty cool." She looked up, then jolted on the floor as if she had dropped something.

"So, dinner," Ovella's mother shouted from behind. Her father, walking behind her, made his way to the kitchen and prepared the dinner table.

I couldn't tell you what they served me that night. Everything from the meat to the desert sounded like a foreign language. I didn't say much as I studied everyone's movements trying to figure out what utensil to use for what meal. I tried mimicking their every move so that I didn't make a fool out of myself; It was important if I wanted to continue seeing Ovella. I'd occasionally look over at her father. I could tell he was studying every movement I was making. He looked like the type that didn't like loud chewing. I tried my best to chew gently and not clink the spoon up against the plates as much.

"So, are you in school?" her mother asked.

"Yea," I said trying my best not to flinch or hesitate as I lied straight to their faces. "I'm attending Washington State University."

"Oh really? What are you majoring in?" She looked over at her husband who was busy chewing on his food. He nodded not bothering to look at me. They didn't seem to notice. "So, what are you majoring in?"

I needed to think quick and before I could think of anything my mouth was already moving, "Civil engineer." She paused and made a little noise with her mouth

"Oh honey," she said placing her hand on his arm. Her father looked up and looked at me for the first time.

"Is Professor Paterson still teaching there?" he asked me.

"Yea, Professor Pat Rat," I said smirking. A large smile grew on his face.

"Professor Pat Rat, that's right."

"His rat finally died, if you're wondering," I said placing my palm on my mouth as I smiled.

"Really, now? That is a shame," I looked over at Ovella. She was looking at me stunned, wondering what was going on.

The remainder of the evening was continued with cheap talk. I didn't say much but answered questions and listened to their simple commentary. I would sometimes look over at Ovella, but she seemed busy eating. I tried my best to seem interested, but I couldn't wait for it all to be over. It wasn't that I felt uncomfortable with them but it was an environment I never really grew up in. I never had to know the difference between eating utensil nor did I ever have to place a napkin on my lap.

"My parents like you," Ovella said the next day at the library.

"Really?"

"So, Professor Pat Rat?" Ovella giggled.

"Yea, the school was recently being renovated and yea. I kinda got around campus," she studied me for a minute.

"I just don't understand. Why'd you lie," she asked me.

"I ah. Like. Ummm," I tried thinking of how to word everything so that she would understand but nothing came out the way I intended it. "Yah know, I just don't think your parents would approve of me."

"My parents don't care. I've dated all sorts of races," she said not fully understanding what I meant. I thought about correcting her and explaining that it wasn't a question of race but a question of education. I wasn't able to look them in the face and tell them that I had dropped out of high school my freshman year because I'm not able to attend any college or university due to my legal status. Someone like me, with no future, has no business talking to a girl like Ovella. My chances would have been ruined before I even got an opportunity with her.

"Well, other than that he likes you. He said, 'I like how he knows how to keep his mouth closed.'" She said mimicking her father's deep voice. "And my mom says you're sweet."

"Well. That's good," I stuttered not knowing how to respond. I felt slightly disappointed having lied, but it was something I couldn't go around. "So, am I the first person your parents like?"

"I mean, everyone else that I bring over can't stop talking. Like, there trying to impress my parents, you know? They brag about their high grades, honor rolls, their acceptance into prestige colleges. You didn't, and they like that."

She picked up a book, as I pulled out a piece of paper and started writing. It had been nearly over a month since I had written anything. Having nearly lost my hand, I was relieved I still had any motor skills. It was painful the first couple words, but I pushed through. Words eventually became sentences, and before the end of the day, I had finished a short story. Ovella wandered over, asking what I had written. Handing it over, she asked if I enjoyed writing. Quickly reading it, she handing it back without telling me what she thought. It bothered me. I wanted to impress her, to show her that I wasn't just a construction worker and that even though I was a high school dropout I could write.

"I think you should go to this workshop," Ovella suggested as I walked her out of the library. I sighed, having a feeling she didn't like my writing. "You need to pursue your dream, Alejandro."

"What do you mean?" I wondered trying to think what my dream was.

"You have a way with words," she said. An image of Hope rendered in my mind. "I think you'll enjoy this workshop I go to at the end of the month. It really helps with my writing, and you'll meet a ton of popular writers. Maybe they can help you."

Writing had become a pleasure of mine as well as a way for me to free myself from everything. I did not see writing as a competitive sport so the idea of becoming a better writer had never crossed my mind. In my mind, I wrote from the heart. Sadly, not everyone saw it that way. The first time I came to the workshop was my last. Listening to people critique other writers bothered me. Surprisingly, I was the only one who saw a problem as everyone quickly jotted down notes and awed in amazement. There seemed to be more editors than writers. I was disgusted by the sight of others being molded to believe that there was a right way of writing. When Ovella insisted that I hand over one of my short stories to a close friend, I was skeptical. Handing it back, his words were, "Its non-realistic. And if you plan on becoming a writer, write about things everyone can relate with." I replied with my half smile.

"So, what you think about the workshop?" Ovella asked me after we left.

"I'm not going back there," I told Ovella.

"Why?" she asked. I didn't respond as I was wondering if it was the right time to ask her to be my girlfriend. "I still think you should go back to school," she said gently.

"I can't."

"I understand that you can't but even if you could. You said you wouldn't go. Why?"

"Because it's not for me. I don't think I fit anymore. Like I don't feel comfortable. I'm more comfortable hanging out with a bunch of grown men. I relate with them more," I said having trouble explaining myself. "And as a writer, I'd be doing myself a favor if I stayed in construction."

"Really," Ovella asked. "Show me! Besides, I'm tired of going to the library. I want a bit of an adventure."

"I don't think that's a good idea."

"Come on! That's not fair. I'ma writer too!" Ovella pouted. I couldn't decide on what to do. I wanted to take her, but I was afraid of what she would think of me afterward. My palms got sweaty knowing that I didn't have much to offer her. But she needed to see who I was, and I needed to know if she would still feel the same way afterward.

Loud Ranchero music was playing outside the apartment complex as everyone sat around a pickup truck drinking. I introduced them to Ovella. I could tell she was shy as none of them spoke English but she made her best introducing herself.

"Una chela?" one of them asked as they pulled out a beer and tried handing it over to Ovella.

"No. no thank you," she kindly declined.

"I wonder who's cooking tonight?" The door was open, and I could smell seasoning. "Hey, Gary! I heard you was giving out boxing lessons?"

"Ohhh, come on cuzn'," Gary laughed stepping out the kitchen and into the living room. "You got jokes today, Aly, hehehe." He paused noticing Ovella. "You didn't say we was havn' visitors. I'm lookin' a mess. The place lookin' a mess. Oh, cuz, why you gotta do me like this?"

"It's all good, Gary," I joked. His golden front tooth shined as he smiled. "Ay, Gary, let me hollah at you for a minute."

"Oh, shit! Was up, cuz?"

"I know somebody that know somebody that know somebody that told me you was cooking tonight."

"Aaaaaghhhhhh, you already know! Tu primo cookin' tonight! Yezir," he said laughing walking back to the kitchen.

"How about them boxin' lessons?"

"Ey, cuzn'," Gary called. I turned around barely catching the beer he had thrown me. Opening it, we walked outside and sat on the curb.

"You see that guy," I pointed at the husky guy leaning up against the truck. "When I first met him, I couldn't stand him. Something about his crooked smile bothered me. I've ever met

147

someone who smiled as much as him and it bothered me. But anyways, when he was young. He went to college to become a tuna tester." Ovella quickly gave me a puzzled look. "I know right," I answered back, already knowing what she was thinking. "It didn't last long anyways. But he went back to school to become a computer programmer, he didn't like it. He said sitting in a chair all day long was not his thing. That's when his wife and him came to the States where he picked oranges for a living. He never had kids, and I don't know if that had anything to do with his wife's illness but. She passed away." I paused having the need to give my respects. "I don't know what it is, but he never let life bring him down. Most people become alcoholics, depressed, hooked on pills. But not him. Every day he wakes up and smiles. His life isn't anything extravagant. It's been sad. But he enjoys the simple things. And that makes life beautiful." I stopped and pointed at another man. "Don Tano over there has a mixed daughter who he hasn't seen in over four years. Last time he saw her was her freshman school dance when he went to pick her up. She said she'd never wanted to see him again. I guess she had told everyone her whole life that her father was black."

"I don't understand why she would do that. I'm mixed, and everyone knows my dad's white and my mom's black."

"It's different. Both your parents are normal Americans with normal jobs. Don Tano is an illegal Columbian that doesn't speak English and digs holes for a living."

"I mean I guess," was all Ovella could say.

"Gary inside. He's like eighty years old, if not older. And believe it or not. He ain't never been married. He ain't got no kids. Nothing. He says that wasn't in God's plan for him. That's crazy to me. His whole life, he's worked and that all he knows." I stopped and looked over at Ovella, who was probably wondering why I was telling her all this. "I wanna tell you a story my father told me about him. Really short story, by the way, but it means a lot to me. He grew up with seven brothers and four sisters and every morning they would all divide this one piece of bread and a small 12-ounce can of coke for breakfast. As a kid, he never saw it as an issue because it wasn't only his family but everyone else as well. When he told me that, I remember realizing that were all hurting in one way or another, but it isn't so bad when we're all hurting together. Anyways, I love writing and I don't think I'll get as much life and poetry as I do here."

"You know, I still think you should go back to school. I know that's not what you wanna hear, but you gotta think about your future," she paused. "There was something you said that made me, just, I was like he would enjoy college. We were in the library, and we were talking about morality. And you said something that really spoke to me. You said I can't word most of it but the last part. Something like, God, how did it go?" she paused trying to think back. I did the same.

"I've done some bad things; I can't say I'm a good person, but I'm not a bad one either. But everything I've done was out of love, and that transcends beyond what's good and evil."

"Yea," she agreed. "I could see you majoring in philosophy or something."

"Yea you really think so?"

"Yea."

"If I had gone to college, I could only imagine my mother's face." I smiled trying to remember my mother's face.

"So, where are your parents?"

"I don't know. You know, it's funny. Back in Mexico, I would sneak out into the city with my older brother to have some drinks, and I wished I never had to go home. I wish I could go home right now to see my parents but I don't even know where there at," I said.

"What do you mean?"

"Some stuff happened I guess. By the time I got to a payphone, the house phone number was disconnected when I tried reaching them."

"You'll find them," Ovella reassured me.

"Be my girlfriend?" I asked bluntly looking straight at her.

"Yea."

"Yea, like yea, yea?"

"Yea," she said smiling. Wrapping her arms around mine, we watched the sun go down in the distance and although the world was dark and cold. I couldn't' help but feel bright and warm.

"You know I have this idea," I said looking up at the night sky. "I have this idea, that the moon doesn't exist unless I'm looking at it. Like for things to exist you have to acknowledge their existence." Ovella looked up at the moon. "But then I wonder about my existence."

Chapter XVI

"So, you sell your art?" Persela asked scrolling through recent text messages with Anthony. All of them had been sent from her with no responses from him. Tapping on her keyboard, she debated if she wanted to text him again. She glanced at Marc who was sitting across from her, painting. He caught her glancing at him and gently smiled. "I don't wanna see your stupid painting," Persela giggled. Since their night together, Marc started a painting inspired by her. With her constant visits, he assumed she was trying to catch a glimpse of it before anyone else. So, whenever she appeared on his front door, he would have her sit across from his studio. Yet sitting across from each other, she could feel his eyes wandering her body, just as his hands did that night. She would not admit it, but she adored being studying by him. She would bite her lower lip and gently run her hands through her hair whenever they both caught each other's eyes. He would smile and look back at his work. She knew he wanted her, but what had happened that night was a one-time deal. She loved Anthony and no one else.

"No, I don't," Marc said softly.

"Why?" Persela asked surprised.

"Because, I'm an artist. I could never sell my art. My art has no price." Marc put his brush down. "This is an art form not a form of art. I practice for self-recognition, not for the recognition of others.

I have yet to meet another artist in this school or any other school," Marc hissed.

"What! There's like artist all over school," Persela said.

"No, there's students who are studying art and the market. They study trends and not their skill or themselves. They paint what others want them to paint. Fuck that! I paint what I want to paint. Anyways, I could never sell my art. How could I sell something I've spent countless hours perfecting? I had this asshole once tell me he'd give me a hundred dollars for one of my painting. He done lost his fuckin' mind." Persela giggled at his comment. He smiled having made her giggle. "All I know is I like to paint, and I like to get better. Honestly, I don't think I'm an artist. I don't understand art or other pieces of artwork but my own. Realist or abstract, I don't care." Marc noticed Persela looking down at her phone again. He grabbed his brush once more and went back to his painting. They both jumped when Persela's phone went off. She quickly answered it without even looking at who was calling. Marc could not help but listen in. It sounded like a female voice on the other line.

"Oh, my God, yes, Mom, I'm doing fine, ok!" Persela said getting off her seat. "Can I call you later, please? Please? I'm sorry I'll try and do better. I've just been busy you know? I can't always call you. Besides there's only so much you can do. I mean, you are on the other side of the country. Anyways, I'll call you later mom," she hung up. Her phone rang again. "Oh, my God, really," she yelled at the phone. "Oh, Helene," Persela said surprised.

Helene was shouting on the other line. "Oh, my God, he left me! Like I already knew that, but it just hit me you know! He'd left me for some time now but now. It's really sunk in, you know? He left me, Persela!" Persela jolted to her feet and made her way to the door realizing Helene was having a panic attack.

"Helene! Helene! I'm coming. Where are you?" Persela demanded. Slamming the door on her way out, Marc was left behind finishing his painting.

"I think it's done," he said signing the painting at the bottom right corner. He carried it to school that same day and hung it for everyone to see.

———

"I don't know what the fuck is wrong with this kid. What's his fuckin' problem? Does he enjoy getting his ass kicked? I had to kick his ass once. I can't believe I'ma have to do it again! And Persela, I don't know what the fuck is going on with her, but I'll deal with her later. Man, what I've been saying this whole time. Hoes are hoes man, swear. Can't find no one loyal." Anthony said talking on his phone.

"I don't know man. Some people just ain't got common sense." Josh said on the other line.

"Anyways, you sure he lives here?" Anthony asked as he stood in front of apartment 205.

"Yea I am."

"The Pool Table Club's already paying off," Anthony said

"You sure you don't want us to handle it?"

"Nah fuck that. I want to handle this piece of shit myself." Hanging up, he furiously knocked on the door. The door opened. Marc had a confused look when he saw Anthony on his doorstep. Marc was ready to welcome Anthony when Anthony grabbed him by the shirt and threw him across the room. He crashed on top of a blank canvas.

"You saw the painting? Did you like it? I think Persela looks great," he said falling to the ground. The painting of Persela popped up in Anthony's mind. He grew angry at the thought of another man having seen Persela naked.

"What's your fuckin problem, man?" Anthony said throwing a tripod across his loft. "You just like fuckin' others people girlfriends?" Anthony reached over. Grabbing a chair, he savagely threw it at Marc. Marc managed to catch it and throw it back. Anthony blocked it. "So, what's your fuckin problem?" he asked rampaging towards Marc.

"YOU! ALL OF YOU!" Marc yelled. Quickly getting up he flung his arm at Anthony's face and landed a powerful punch on is cheek bone. He tackled him and held him down. "You're all fucking disgusting. You don't think I don't know about you and Tatyana. I actually know Tatyana. You of all people can't be talking about respect. You all fuckin' disgust me. Pretending to like each other. Pretending to be happy when you're all fuckin miserable. At least, I admit it! All of you, aimlessly living with no direction and having the nerve to expect yourselves to end up somewhere! Besides, I don't know why painting Persela is such a big fuckin' deal. When you go behind her back and fuck every other girl that comes your way!" Anthony pushed him off and grabbed a canvas. He swung it at Marc. Marc caught it and snatched it off his hands. "Your boyfriend Josh isn't here to help you now."

"Fuck you!" Anthony swung at him until he landed a clean punch.

"So, did you like it?" Marc asked again as Anthony wrapped his hands around his throat. He gave Anthony a disturbingly satisfied look. "Oh man, I didn't sleep with her if that's what you're wondering. I'm not like you," Marc lied. "She wanted to, though. She had never been adored or touched the way I was touching her," Marc stopped, trying to loosen Anthony's grip. Regaining air, he continued. "I explored her body. I know more about her than you do. You know her hip bone is a tickle spot?" Marc coughed then laughed. Anthony finally released him and walked out his apartment.

———

Anthony was making his way back to his dorm when Persela showed up out of nowhere. He was furious but in control. He wanted to confront Persela but did not. He admitted that Marc was right. He didn't care for Persela. Yet he wondered why he felt bothered?

"Hey, babe," she said, and like a cat wanting attention, rubbing her head on his shoulder. "So, how's your day been?" she asked gently.

"Busy, so where have you been?" he said shaking her off his shoulder.

"I've been with Helene these past couple of days, why didn't you tell me Josh had broken up with her! She's been pretty upset. How about you come over to my dorm tonight?" she finally insisted. He didn't respond. Instead, he tucked his hands in his pockets. "Come on babe. It's been a while since I've had you. I'm kinda craving you right now to be honest." Persela said as she bumped Anthony's hip with her own. She bit her lower lip and winked at him. Anthony completely stopped and began grating his teeth.

"Persela, I have more important things to be doing," Anthony snapped. He wanted to confront here about her affair with Marc, but it didn't matter. And although Marc had told him they had not slept with each other, he was still upset about the whole ordeal. He tried looking at Persela, but he was disgusted. An image of Marc and her came to mind.

Persela stood awestruck. "What's the matter, baby?" She reached over to hold his hand and before she could, Anthony's hand was tightly wrapped around her wrist. He thought about hitting her but stopped before doing so. She stood petrified. "Anthony, let go," she stuttered.

"Fuck off, Persela," Anthony hissed. "You're really starting to piss me off." Anthony's phone rang. He managed to look at it without Persela noticing who it was.

Tatyana: There's a party tonight at Philips.

Anthony: *ok. meet you there. or come pick you up*

"Now, I gotta go," Anthony said finally releasing Persela's hand. "I'll come see you tonight if I get the chance." Anthony said while texting Tatyana back. "Yea, I gotta go but I'll meet you at your dorm tonight."

Persela stood there. Watching Anthony walk away, she felt horrible for how Anthony had treated her. She wondered if it had been something she had said or done. She re-played their conversation trying to spot something she missed. *Maybe I'll go see Helene until tonight*, Persela said to herself.

Helene was inside, laying on her back and lighting up a cigarette when Persela walked in. She stood by Helene's bedroom doorstep not knowing what to say.

"I think you need this more than I do," Helene suggested.

"No, I'm fine."

"God. Persela you're so lucky. You know that, right?" Helene said.

"Why? I don't really feel lucky."

"You have someone. Someone that really loves you."

"You really think so? Sometimes it doesn't feel that way."

"Yea! You and Anthony are so perfect together. Promise me you'll be with him forever. For me. Seeing you both together makes me so happy."

"I know right! We do make a pretty cute couple."

"So tonight," Helene started. "There's a party. I got invited, and we haven't gone out in such a long time. So, I think we need to go. It's going to be the party of the century. We need to go! There's gonna be so many cute boys."

"I don't' know Helene," Persela said thinking of Anthony.

"Do it for me Persela. We'll go for a bit and leave. I just want to get out again!" Helene said practically begging.

"Ok, we'll just go for an hour, not too long. Anthony said he was meeting me back at my dorm tonight. So, I don't wanna be out

156

more then I should." Persela said with seriousness in her tone. Helene got up and disappeared behind her closet.

Chapter XVII

Persela giggled at the sight of all the people arriving to the enormous house that stood on the outskirts of the university. Making their way inside, she noticed two bodyguards near the front door. She wondered if they were going to I.D. her but didn't. Inside, the lights were off, and dub-step music was being played by a DJ, who was set up in the living room.

"Helene," yelled a voice from the crown. A slimy brunet boy approached them with two plastic red cups in his hands.

"Thanks," Helene said being handed both cups "Here take this one Persela," Helene said handing the other.

"Anything you need, let me know? Mi casa is your casa," he said walking away.

"Is this really his house?" asked Persela. "Or does it belong to his parents?"

"I don't know. He's just the guy I go to now since Josh wants to be an asshole," Helene answered smiling.

Persela turned her attention to the dancing crowd. She bit her lower lip. She looked over at Helene. Softly, Persela rubbed her shoulder on Helene's, suggesting that they join the dance floor.

"You know you want to, Helene," Persela suggested.

"You know it bitch," Helene said smiling. "Come on finish your drink so we can do dance." Persela chugged what was left in the cup and tossed it away. Helene grabbed Persela's hand and pulled her to the dance floor. They giggled like small children. Pushing through the crowd, they reached the center of the dance floor. Helene raised her arms in the air and screamed in joy. Persela did the same. She was glad seeing her friend smile. Persela giggled as the music stopped, the crowd roared as they demanded more music.

"Yah, ready to get this party started?!" screamed the DJ into his microphone as the crowd quickly screamed in agreement. The lights came on, and Persela looked around in confusion expecting something to happen. She looked through the crowd and to the backyard. People were in swimming shorts and bikinis, cheering and screaming out to the DJ for more music. Someone jumped into the pool. "Yah, ready for the party of the year?!" asked the DJ as the lights finally went out. Still no music played but instead neon lights and rays of different colors shined around the living room. A cloud of smoke than immersed from the floor as Persela heard a faint beat rising. The beat got louder and louder as some people started to dance again as others continued to cheer and scream in joy. Then out of nowhere, and without warning, the beat went to its max, it shook the house and made Persela jump to her feet. Being pushed around by insane dancers, she quickly rejoined the dancing. She closed her eyes for a split second and just as she opened them Helene had disappeared.

Concerned, she left the crowd to search for her. She entered the kitchen, where a group of people were. She sat on top the granite table and pulled her phone out. She texted Helene and Anthony. Waiting for a response, she eavesdropped on a group's conversation.

"Bro, were gonna have so much fun tonight."

"Yea, man, those pills are on another level, man."

"Yea, man! I'm really feeling it. This shit's awesome."

That's when her phone buzzed. She looked and saw it was Anthony replying to her text.

Persela: *Hey babe.*

Anthony: *I won't be seeing you tonight i'm feeling sick.*

Persela felt slightly disappointed but was glad she had come to the party now. She jumped off the counter top table as one of the boys approached her.

"Hey," he said softly. He had blood red eyes and a cocky smirk. He looked Persela up and down before continuing his conversation. "You want to come chill with us?" he mumbled.

"Sorry, hun. I wish I could, but I gotta go find my friend. But how about you give me your drink," Persela said in her notorious flirtatious voice.

"Oh, this drink," said the red-eyed boy as he raised the cup he was holding. "Yea, yea you can have it." He handed it over. "Let me refill it for you," he turned around to his friends and refilled it. Receiving the cup, she took a small sip.

"Thanks, cutie. We should hang out some time though." Persela said as she started walking away.

"Yea, yea fo show," said the boy.

She searched the entire house for Helene and after exploring every room and corner, she was nowhere to be seen. Stepping outside she felt the coolness of the night run up her skin. Walking by the pool, she looked into the water and saw her reflection. It was blurry and out of focus. She focused hard on seeing herself, but that only worsened her vision. A splash of water hit her face after someone jumped in it. Laughing, she looked down at her drink and noticed it was empty. That's when it hit her like a ton of bricks. She began to feel dizzy, and everything around her seemed to be turning upside down. Her knees felt weak and before she fell into the pool someone caught her.

"You alright?" someone said. She looked up at the person's but couldn't see their face properly.

"Yea," she mumbled. "I'm fine. Let go of me. I just need to sit down."

Every wall spun uncontrollably when she stepped back inside. Trying to get upstairs, she bumped her way through the crowd of people dancing. Everyone's face seemed distorted.

Persela found an empty room. Laying down on the bed she closed her eyes yet focused on staying awake. That's when she felt someone's touch. It felt like Anthony's hand on her color bone. She smiled and opened her eyes to see someone else on top of her. It was the boy who had given up his drink in the kitchen. She wanted him to get off but with both her hands being held down, she could not move. Scared and helpless, Persela trembled in fear for the first time in her life. She struggled but managed to set herself free. Frustrated with Persela's resistance, he punched her in the face. Persela froze and submitted to his desires.

"Help," she whispered.

"Yea, baby, I'm here. Help's already here," he whispered as his left hand caressed her collar bone.

"Help," Persela whimpered again. She looked up towards the door hoping someone would come rescue her.

"Is this room busy?" someone asked opening the door. Persela lost her breath hearing Anthony's voice. She couldn't help but break out in tears.

"Baby," Persela said faintly.

"Oh, man, what! Is this your girl?" asked the boy. He quickly got off. Anthony entered the room where he saw Persela with another man.

"Nah, bro, that bitch ain't mine," Anthony said with a disgusted look on his face.

"Let's go find another room, babe," Tatyana said. She reached her hand over Anthony's shoulder and kissed his neck. Anthony reached the door handle and shut it.

"No," Persela begged. The stranger jumped back on her. His blood red eyes looked more menacing than before. Persela looked around the room looking for something she could use to her advantage. She saw a wardrobe that held a heavy looking television. Then a closet. Quickly, she squirmed from his grip and crawled towards it. The stranger reached for her leg. Persela turned around and kicked him off. She jolted to the closet afraid of being beaten. She opened the door and hid inside. Her hands held on tightly to the door knob. She could feel him tugging at it, but Persela held on tight. Her face felt hot, she could feel it swelling up. As she held on to the door knob with one hand, she attempted to contact someone from her phone. She called Helene. No answer. She tried calling Josh. No answer. The boy from the other side pulled on the door again. The door slightly opened. Persela dropped her phone and managed to close the door before he could get inside.

"I'm not gonna hurt you! It's a fuckn' party. Let's have some fun!"

Persela ignored him. Reaching down to her now broken phone, she saw a contact she did not recognize. "Leo." Picking up her phone, she called the stranger named Leo. The phone rang twice when someone answered.

"Please," Persela cried. "I'm at...Avondale Estates on Jackson St." The boy tugged the door once more and finally opened it.

Chapter XVIII

September 17, 2012
Everyone dies, but nothing hurts more than not
speaking to someone that's still alive

"Well, that was interesting," I said looking out the car window. Ovella looked over at me then back at the road.

"Honestly, did you like it?"

"Yea, I did. I'm just not used to going to dances or meetings like that," I tried explaining myself. I looked back at Ovella and then turned my attention back to the passing cars.

"It's a good idea attending these kinds of events. It gives you the opportunity to network with important people who have leverage. You know what I mean?" she tried explaining it once more like it wasn't something I'd already heard.

"I mean it was fine. I just don't like the way they look at me."

"What do you mean?"

"Nothing, I just heard what your principal said about me."

"I'm so sorry you had to hear that. God, I hate how she can be sometimes. You know I could tell that you were upset. You give this half smile."

"Yea, I've been told," I replied.

***

I was awkwardly walking around a group of people who were conversing about something important. Most of them turned around and gave me the kind of look that suggested I wasn't welcomed. Not that I had any intentions of joining, I was just curious if Ovella was within that group. I eventually found her with her principal talking to a group of men. I could tell Principal Kimberly admired them as her eyes never roamed elsewhere. She remained focused to whoever was speaking. Laughing at a ridiculous joke, she smoothly ran her hand down one of theirs arms. I didn't bother entering their discussion as it had something to do with the upcoming election.

"I really do truly believe he's going to win. He has to. For the well-being of this nation. For the greater good."

"That's great and all, but one things being a business man and another is being the president."

"What do you think, Ovella?" someone asked.

"I don't think someone filled with hate and xenophobia should be given so much power. He's talking about banning an entire group of people and registering everyone who practically isn't white," Ovella responded.

"What do you think Alejandro," Principle Kimberly asked me. "These are your people, right?" Someone chuckled within the group.

"I'm not worried," I said.

"Classic, Alejandro," Principle Kimberly said. "He's so carless about everything. Even with his own life," she said with a small grin. Everyone else did the same.

"It'll be his fault," I said cutting everyone off. "When someone more cruel and evil comes into existence."

"Ovella, so where does your boyfriend, Alejandro, plan on going?" Principal Kimberly asked trying to change the topic.

"He is, umm, not going to college, Principal Kimberly," Ovella said looking down at the cup she was holding.

"Not going to college," Mrs. Kimberly said placing her hand on her chest. "You know Ovella." She glanced over at the other men. "Here are some fine gentlemen."

"Anyways it was a pleasure meeting everyone," I said reaching out to shake Principle Kimberly's hand. She looked down and frowned in disgust. Ignoring my scarred hand, she reached over and patted me on my shoulder.

"Yes, of course."

***

"I'ma start wearing gloves," I said.

"But you know, you need to try and do something. You need to go to college somehow. I mean of course after you finish High School." Ovella said disregarding my comment.

"You know I can't," I said not wanting to turn around.

"Well, do something! Don't just sit there and feel bad for yourself." I finally turned around and looked at her. "I love you, and you know this. I want you to stop thinking nothing is possible in the world."

"I can't. I'm illegal. I'm happy with you and you're all I want. No one cares who I am or what I am. I have no money, and the money I do have isn't enough. I can't afford a lawyer."

"No, Alejandro, you can do something about it, and I wish you'd see it. You just need to stop thinking so negative about it. I believe in you, and I know you were raised being told that hard work is the only way to live, but sometimes that's not good enough. I grew up being told when you want something, you have to take it and when someone wants to take it away, you fight for it," Ovella spoke passionately. I admired every word she spoke. It was hard to believe that someone cared for me so much and saw something in me that I couldn't. "I know you had or still have dreams of doing something more than this. Whatever your dream is, don't ever forget it or ever let go of it and do whatever it takes to get it. I mean college is a good thing. Construction is ok, but having to struggle to find work the way you do. It doesn't really provide a sense of security, you know." I bit my lower lip trying not to protest. I looked away so she couldn't see my frustration. "There's more to you then this. I wish you could see half of what I see in you."

"Yea?"

"So, there is something I need to tell you."

"Kevin, the guy who were just talking with," she said. I could already hear what she was going to say.

"Yea, what about him?" I said waiting for her to finish.

"Just as we were leaving, he called me over and said he needed to tell me something," Ovella stopped in mid-sentence as she pulled into my apartment complex. Slowly she pulled into a parking lot and parked.

"What did he tell you," I said. She turned the engine off.

"He leaned in and kissed me."

"Like in the mouth," I said calmly.

"No, as a saw him. He leaned in. I turned around. He kissed me on the cheek," Ovella waited for me to respond. I said nothing.

"What do you think?" I said plainly.

"I don't know," Ovella said. She laughed. "I guess it doesn't really matter since I'll be leaving tomorrow."

"Yea," I said. Ovella's phone buzzed. I managed to catch a glimpse and see it was Kevin.

"I'm going to the restroom. I'll be back," Ovella said placing her phone back in the car's cup holder.

"No one is home, right?"

"No, they all went out to the bar," I explained as Ovella stepped out her car.

I looked over at her phone. I thought about grabbing her phone and sending him my address. Without a doubt, he would think it was Ovella inviting him over. I imagined my hands wrapping around his throat. But just as I was ready to text in my address, I stopped.

"Thanks for the party invitation," I said when Ovella returned. We stood outside her car staring at each other, wanting more time. "You know I'm gonna be driving from here on out."

"Yea," Ovella said displeased. She looked to her side. "Just be careful. I don't want to get a phone call from someone telling me you're getting deported," Ovella said seriously but then laughed.

"I'll try."

"I have to get going," Ovella said sadly. "I want to spend some time with my family. You know I'll always love you, right?" Ovella said looking at me with her butterfly like eyes.

"And I'll always love you," I said wanting to say more but nothing ever came. In a couple words, I wanted to say something that could explain the way I felt about her. *And I'll always love you.* The phrase repeated and I wondered if that was enough.

———

"Let me call you back. I'm a lil busy," Ovella would tell me at almost every attempt to contact her. Weeks passed and I tried my best to keep in contact with her. It was always either some important orientations, club meetings, and lunch with classmates. Honestly, it never bothered me. But I'd be lying if I said I wasn't hurting. My heart ached when my phone calls starting going to voicemail. Afraid that I'd lose her, I wanted to promise her everything. But I remembered what my mother once told me, "son live your life but when you find someone you love. Don't make promises you can't keep." So just like that, I never called her again. I grew this idea that she was afraid of loving me. I thought of becoming someone, something greater so that she'd love me without fear. I promised myself that the next time we would meet, I would be someone.

Chapter XIX

December 18, 2014

Dear, Mrs. Deborah

I want to first thank you for everything you did for me and apologize as well. I have to come clean as it has been bothering me for years. If I remember correctly, I had a report on self-honesty.

I think being self-honest is one of the hardest things an individual can do, but it is necessary for growth. When I met you, I lied. I was no high school student. I don't have a logical or good enough reason to have lied to you, but I feel horrible having done so. I want to apologize for having wasted your time writing all those pointless papers and reports on books. I feel guilty having stolen a student's teacher. I was and still am a construction worker and nothing more. That is the truth and now having admitted it I can finally grow. I can finally let go of my childish dream of becoming a writer and other fairy tales alike and truly focus on maturing into adulthood.

Sincerely, Alejandro L. D.

P.S. I am doing fine, all is well. I hope the same goes for you. Met a girl, she's nice. I think I'm ok with that.

Chapter XX

May 24, 2016
God is good and God is evil

I was getting back from work when I saw a luxurious car parked outside my apartment complex. I pulled up next to it. The chrome shined liked it had never been driven. I tried looking inside when I stepped out but couldn't see past its tinted windows. I didn't think much about it as I walked up the steps. Reaching my apartment, I noticed someone standing next to the door. It was an old man wearing a black suit. I wanted to step back down the stairs and make it seem as if I had forgotten something, but it was too late. The man noticed me and was looking straight at me. I thought about running, but for what? I hadn't done anything. Had I?

"Can I help you?" I asked. The man smiled and looked at me.

"Ms. Emerson would like to see you," the man said with a smile that wrinkled his nose. The name sounded familiar, but no face came to mind. I wondered if he had the wrong person. Noticing my front door ajar, I stepped inside. There she was, sitting on the living room couch glancing through the pages of my journal.

"Ah, the man I've been looking for," Ms. Emerson said getting up. She looked me up and down. "You're not exactly what I imagined. I see what Johnny was talking about." She was an elderly woman with dreadlocks that came down to her lower back. "So, you like to write. That's nice," she said throwing my journal on the couch.

"I do," I said not knowing exactly how to respond.

"But, tell me this. You have sections. Some parts talk about peace and love. Very pretty. Very spiritual. Yet on every other page it's filled with war and hate? Completely two different philosophical perspectives, don't you think?"

I was beginning to grow agitated. I thought about telling her to get the fuck outta my house but what came out was, "because that's the truth." A smile grew on the old lady's face. I could tell she was waiting for an explanation. "That peace and war exist. That hate and love exist. That life and death exist. That they coexist and exist because of each other's presence and if that's how the universe works then that's how I should too."

"My child, but why?"

"I don't know," I looked away trying to find the answer somewhere in my living room. "I guess I'm hoping to find answers."

"Child and I will give them to you," Ms. Emerson looked at me then at my apartment. "So, I'm sure your wondering why I'm here," she frowned in disgust. "So, you're the boy. You know I've heard a lot about you?" She looked back at me with disappointment in her eyes. "You know it's a sin to waste talent. And clearly, you've been wasting your time pretending to be something you're not. Come on now. You won't be needing anything."

Chapter XXI

When he appeared, he joined the world's disorder and desolation. He engulfed this dismantled world like a thick morning fog. No one feared him until he spoke and the ground shook.

"I will conquer the world and to those who defy me, I will not hesitate."

Terrifying events unfolded as if the universe had aligned perfectly for this great disaster. With no flaw and only perfection, God's wrath was to blame.

"For I will be your God."

His unstoppable will engulfed everything into darkness and when a glimmering light appeared it was only a blazing fire.

And out of the fire, turmoil, and blood, he was the kind of man who enjoyed watching everything turn to ashes. Nor money, power, or control could win him over. So, as the world was surrendered to him, he held it gently on his palms.

"For I am now and forever will be, Leo the Great and Terrible."

The world was finally his.

Chapter XXII

Frieda Fichel was old but, having been raised in Germany's countryside, never accepted being too old to work. Despite moving to a completely new country with her daughter and ten-year-old granddaughter, she relentlessly looked for a job in the United States. With the little English she knew, she managed to get around easily but being elderly, she could not convince anyone that she could work. She never gave up hope, and like she always did, she prevailed. She found herself with a job where they were specifically looking for a German speaking maid or butler who could cook, clean, or wash. Frieda contemplated the offer. The pay was more than Frieda needed but there was the condition that if she got the job, she would have to live on the estate. She thought about not being able to see her granddaughter grow and then thought about her daughter. She hated watching her struggle just to support the two of them. She felt guilty about not being able to provide at least for herself and, although her daughter never admitted that her own mother was a load, she could see her growing tired every day. With her unable able to find work and her daughter working two shifts, she spent most of her time with her baby grand-daughter. She was grateful at first, but it felt wrong. It should have been the other way around. Frieda felt that she was robbing her daughter of motherhood. In the end, Frieda decided to apply to the estate.

She called the estate and with the simple fact that she spoke German, Frieda was accepted on the spot. The next day, a chauffeur arrived at the apartment complex to escort her to the castle.

"Momma, you do not have to work."

"I do. And you must focus on being a mother." Frieda protested. Frieda knew there was nothing she could say to convince her daughter that she needed and wanted to work. "It will only be for some time." With a gentle wave and a kiss on the baby's forehead she got into the car. She thought about her family the entire ride towards the countryside.

Finally, entering a gate and following a path lined with oak trees, a three-story snow white mansion appeared in the distance. It grew larger the closer they got to it. With Roman columns surrounding the villa, she wondered what God resided there.

Astonished at the inside, Freida gave herself the grand tour. The white marble floor glittered like diamonds as did the golden Victorian chandeliers that hung from the arched ceiling. Stepping lightly down the large corridor she admired the painted ceiling. Everywhere she looked up she found a baby angel giggling behind a cloud. She was completely speechless. There was not a word that could explain how much she respected the estate's beauty. Everything shined in gold and smelled like spring as every window and door was kept open. She was deep inside the house when she felt a gentle breeze pass by her. It reminded her of how beautiful the world she lived in was. She made her way to the back not expecting to see a botanical garden. She was ready to lose herself within the garden when a butler approached her and handed her the key to her room. Her room was nothing less than she expected. She felt like royalty lying under exotic silk covers. She had found heaven and God was nowhere to be seen.

Her job was not as demanding as she had imagined it to be. A week had passed, and all she did on a regular basis was dust the paintings and the countless vases that were in every room on every floor except the third floor. And in the week that passed, not once had she met the owner. Unfortunately, he was away on a trip, and no one knew when to expect a return. In the meantime, Frieda made her acquaintance with everyone that worked there; they were all from different regions of the world. They each spoke their native tongues but spoke enough English to communicate with each other. And just like Frieda, they were clueless to who lived in the large estate. After a month, she began to feel uneasy not having returned to her family. With no phone line, she had to wrote letters to her daughter.

That same month, she received her first paycheck of ten thousand dollars. Shocked, she felt that there was a mistake, but who could she report it to? She would have to wait for the owners to get home. Frieda mailed the check to her daughter, not having any need for it. Within the house, every necessity to live was taken care of. Unlike her daughter, she did not have to pay for rent or groceries. As hard as it was for her, she admitted the job was promising.

It was the middle of the night when Frieda heard a loud bang coming from the front door. Frightened, she jolted to her feet. Grasping her chest, she felt her heart beat rampaging up against her rib cage. For a second, she thought the house was being robbed. She made her way downstairs to the front yard to find no one and no signs of a broken entry. She waited for others to walk downstairs but they never did. No one else seemed to have heard it but her. As she lay back down and looked out the window, a tree branch danced as the wind blew. *The wind must have knocked something over,* she thought.

The following morning, someone noticed four suitcases left near the spiral staircase that led to the third floor. The king had returned to his palace. Frieda wished she had seen the arrival. An unfamiliar energy came over the house as everyone panicked to cook a delicious morning breakfast. They all sat waiting for someone to come down but no one ever did. They sat quietly hearing the third-floor creaking. The remainder of that day was eerie as everyone stayed on the lookout for an appearance but whoever had arrived spent the entire day on the third-floor walking about.

Freida had a hard time sleeping when she finally headed to bed. She tossed and turned trying to ignore the owner's presence, but the creaking continued all night. She rose as the sun was rising. A bird was chirping on a tree branch as a wild cat crawled from behind it. The wind blew, brushing the leaves and scaring the bird away. The sun's warm rays lit her forehead and reached her fragile eyes causing her to look down. That's when she heard the third floor. It shook like an earthquake. She could hear a door being swung open and someone running quickly down the stairs. He ran outside, pushing the front door so hard it hit the wall and created the loud banging noise she had heard the night before. A figure ran towards the gates at full speed as if chasing someone or running from something. She looked down at a wild cat, who jumped through a window on the third-floor balcony. *I need to get it before it makes a mess*, she thought. Walking upstairs, she heard the cat purring. A piece of glass shattered behind the door.

She knew no one was allowed upstairs, but it could not be helped. Inside, she saw no heavenly room or the Sistine Chapel. The walls weren't made of gold and paintings didn't hang from them. Instead, the air was filled with torn papers soaring freely in the air, countless books in different languages, an open luggage bag, and strangely no bed. She looked down on a piece of paper on the floor. The name Beatrice was written on it.

When Frieda found the cat, it was on top a birdcage, attempting to eat the bird that was inside. Frieda quickly grabbed the intruder by the scruff of its neck and launched it out the window. It screeched all the way down.

She was walking out the room when a young man walked in. He was standing in front of her confused as to what she was doing in his room. He wore a red silk wardrobe. He was nothing Frieda had imagined. She had imagined him being an old white man. Instead, he was a young brown-skinned boy, no older than her own daughter. He smoothly placed his hands behind him and lowered his head.

"I sorry for the mess," he said in horrible German. He walked passed her and setting down a black leather journal, walked towards the birdcage. He grabbed the bird from inside the cage and released it out the window.

"Should I have this room cleaned?" Frieda asked in English.

"No, it's fine." He looked over the balcony. "Please speak to me in Germany. I have to learn. I'm so sorry. I hope I did not wake you," the young prince said in German as he turned to Frieda. Frieda was ready to explain it was not his fault and that it was all right when he started talking again. "I have this dream. Or memory. I think. It seems so real. I'm supposed to let go of the past but it seems to haunt me. So, I have this dream or memory. So, when I wake up and find myself here. I run. I run towards her. I run towards Beatrice. You see I'm trying to remember." He tapped himself on the forehead. "When was her birthday?" Frieda looked at him not knowing what to say.

"I'll make some tea," was all she said.

"Blue, I think that was her favorite color. Yea! NO! I remember her saying something about red."

"Master, please relax," Frieda pleaded. He frantically turned around and seeing a pair of black gloves, put them on as he retrieved his black leather journal and held it tightly around his chest.

"You have to come with me. Her gravestone in here. I brought her here," he grabbed Frieda's hand and led her downstairs. He stopped on the bottom step and looked up at the ceiling before arriving at the botanical garden where there was a gravestone marked, Beatrice. "I don't. I can't. I can't remember anything about her." Frieda's master pulled out his journal and starting writing. Finishing he turned around and looked up at Frieda, "I used to be able to write so well."

"Hmm," was all Frieda could say as she stood there next to her master waiting for him to finish and accompany him back to his estate. She could not help but notice that every sentence that started in his journal began with the name Beatrice. She wondered who she was but never asked. He shook his head and quickly erased what he had just written.

181

This was a dear memory for Frieda. It was the day she met Leo.

Chapter XXIII

"My dear, Leo, you should not play with a girl's heart," explained Frieda as she took a sip of her tea.

"I did nothing. It was she who played with it," remarked Leo. Agitated, he too took a sip of his tea. Frieda noticed his gloves. She always thought he looked ridiculous in them but never made a comment. "Besides, as you recall, she boasted about how it was impossible for her to fall in love. And I liked that about her. Sadly, that's the kind of girl I need."

"My child, she was a beautiful being," Frieda commented.

"I don't think I deserve anyone," Leo replied. "I'm actually glad this happened."

"My child, you cannot deprive yourself of love. Love is something difficult but in the end. In the end, it is worth the pain." Frieda sighed. "Will I live to see you marry?" Frieda said laughing and then thought of saying, *Or, at least, see you without those horrible gloves on?* but did not.

"I can promise that you will live to see your two-hundredth birthday, but I cannot promise that you will see me marry."

"So, are you excited? It's almost that time of the year," Frieda said ignoring Leo's statement.

"I am," Leo said giving his large smile. That's when Leo's phone rang.

"Who could that possibly be at this time?" Frieda said concerned. Her facial expression then changed. "My sweet Leo," Frieda said with a smirk on her face. "Is that someone whom you've been hiding from me? Please go on. Ignore my presence and answer," she said brushing her right hand in the air, urging him on.

Leo blushed at her comment and, being somewhat embarrassed, looked away as he answered. Frieda examined Leo's face as she heard a women's voice on the other line. She grew concerned seeing his face quickly grow serious and menacing. He hung up and rudely got up.

"Leo, is everything ok?" Frieda said, also getting up.

"My dearest friend, I must leave for a short time. Please do not worry."

Leo jolted through his mansion, wishing he had a smaller home. Reaching his garage filled with luxurious cars he got inside the nearest one.

"Master Leo!" someone screamed. "I am your chauffeur. What is the meaning of this?" he explained as he approached Leo.

Leo's window rolled down, his chauffeur attempted to open the door, but Leo had locked it.

"Am I not your driver, Master Leo? Now please unlock the door and allow me to do my job."

"You are, but for tonight, you are excused. Please, do me a grand favor and tell everyone inside to prepare a large dinner for a guest I am picking up," explained Leo.

Leo drove off his palace and disregarded every stop sign and red light. Reaching under his seat, he pulled out a 9mm and placed it on his lap. He grabbed his phone and called the number. It went straight to voicemail.

"Heyyyy, this is Persela speaking. I'm either busy with schoolwork or with Anthony. So, text me because I don't read voicemails. Bye."

He ran through his contacts and called Philip.

"Yea," Philip said answering.

"Hey, I know it's late but I need something done right now. I'm going to send you this phone number. I need you to track the location and send it to me. Right now." He hung up. It wasn't long before he was sent an address.

He drove into the neighborhood and reached Jackson Street. He could hear the music and chaos coming from the party. Stepping out from his car he tucked the pistol behind him.

Leo walked inside. With everyone dancing or socializing, no one noticed him. He checked the entire house, inside and out. He thought back to the phone call. He had heard someone trying to get in from outside somewhere. *She must be inside somewhere hiding*, he thought. Up the stairs, there was a door being guarded by two teenagers. He attempted walking past them, but one of them put his hand on Leo's chest, suggesting he was not allowed in.

"Room's busy, bruh."

Leo looked down at the kid's hand and without warning pulled out his gun.

"Move," Leo said as the teenager jerked his hand back.

Leo opened the door, still gripping his gun. Someone laid on top Persela's naked body. Her face was bruised and horribly smeared with make-up and tears.

"Loos'n the fuck up. Enjoy yourself, bitch." Leo took his gun and tapped it on the door. Persela's violator stopped and looked over his shoulder. Upset at Leo's intrusion, he quickly got up and approached him. Not noticing the gun, he grabbed Leo by his blazer and tried to lift him off his feet, but failed.

"Room's busy, asshole," he said. Leo ignored his comment. His attention was at Persela's helpless naked body. A swooshing noise flew through the room. The boy quickly released Leo and dropped to the floor in agony. He grabbed his foot then let out a scream.

Concealing his weapon, Leo walked over to Persela's scattered clothing and handed them back to her. She snatched them from Leo's hand and held them tight against her breasts. Leo looked back to the boy who had just raped Persela. He wanted to kill him, but he held the urge of pulling the trigger between his eyes. He looked back at Persela. She was lying on the bed in fetal position. She was crying and holding on tightly to her belongings. Putting his blazer around her, he reached over and picked her up. A crowd of people ran upstairs but turned back after seeing blood on the bedroom floor.

"Who do you think you are crashing into someone's party?" Anthony demanded. He was waiting at the bottom of the stairs. Leo didn't respond as he made his way down the steps. "You're not leaving with her. I don't know who you think you fuckn' are but you came to the wrong party to pull some shit like that," Anthony said menacingly. Leo recognized Anthony's face. He had seen him the same day he found Persela in the city street. Leo wondered what Anthony was doing. He knew that, from that night, he didn't care about Persela's well-being. Leo gently pushed past him and was making his way to the door when Anthony jumped in front of him with a gun pointed in his face. Leo stopped. A grin appeared on Anthony's face. That's when Leo leaned in and pressed his forehead up against the barrel. Leo face was calm. Unlike, Anthony's, who was growing frustrated. Anthony had never shot a man, let alone killed one. He was now in a situation he had not expected. The entire scene had played out differently in his head. Everyone waited for Anthony's next move. He started to grind his teeth in frustration.

Everything froze. The music stopped, and all the excitement ceased. Everyone stared as Anthony held the gun at Leo's forehead. Anthony turned to the crowd, "This is none of your business!" Leo took this opportunity. In a single motion, Leo kicked Antony's left knee cap in. Anthony collapsed, gasping for air.

"Next time you point a gun at someone already have the intention of shooting them."

Leo carried Persela to his car and gently placed her in the back seat. "It's ok. It's ok now. Go ahead and get dressed." Leo said gently.

"Please just get me out of here," Persela pleaded as she crawled to the far corner of the car. Having been looked and treated like an object, she wanted to disappear far away from everyone. She gripped on tightly to her belongings, trying to remember who she was. She tightly closed her eyes, hoping that when she opened them, she would be back home. But no matter how many times she tried she was still there, miserable and destroyed inside. She looked at the man who had rescued her. He was outside the car standing by the car door.

"I don't think I ever properly introduced myself. My name is Leo," Leo said stepping back in. "If it will make you feel any better I can hand the gun over to you," Leo said with a smile on his face. Persela was silent. She tucked her knees in and stared out the window instead.

"Please, just get me out of here," she pleaded again.

Persela watched the house party disappear behind her. The further away they drove off, the more she wanted the horrific event to disappear with it. But it had happened, and there was nothing she could do to change that. She tried not thinking about it and made every effort to distract herself from it. She looked out the car and counted every tree they drove by. When they stopped at a red street light, she focused all her attention on how long it stayed red before turning green. She looked over at a woman driving next to them. The woman sped up. Persela went back to counting every tree that passed them. Eventually, she grew tired and without realizing, fell into a deep sleep.

Persela awoke to the car shaking. She looked out the window and saw countless oak trees that looked identical to the next. She turned to the window shield and saw a magnificent mansion that was brightly lit.

Leo drove into the garage where a row of servants stood waiting. They all carried a worried look on their faces.

"Can someone please bring me a blanket," Leo demanded as he stepped out. Someone rushed inside. Everyone else waited eagerly to see who was inside the car. When he was handed the blanket, he looked at all his servants. "Everyone is dismissed but can someone call forth Frieda!" Leo demanded. He walked over the car and wrapped the blanket over Persela's naked body. "You know I've been trying to get something off my chest for some time now," Leo started. "Nothing happened between me and you that night. I'm pretty sure you know that but… Just one of those things I want to tell you. I know this isn't the best time to be telling you this but. Yea. Just something I've wanted to tell you. Oh and. I know my hands aren't pretty. That's why I wear gloves," Leo said waving his right hand in the air. That was when Frieda stormed in.

"My Dear Leonidas, do not ever leave the house in that matter," Frieda said. "Thank the heavens you have returned fine." She looked inside the car and noticed Persela. "My lord, she is a beautiful creature. An angel from the heaven! I will personally tend to this fallen angel."

"Please tend to her," Leo said walking away.

"What is your name, my dear?"

"Persela," Persela whispered.

"I am Frieda." Frieda noticed a small bruise on her cheek bone. She looked away trying to not have noticed it. "Well come on. Cover yourself. I don't want you getting a cold.

———

"This will be your room," Frieda said as she opened the door. It was a large room with black marble flooring and a large round bed in the middle. Red and pink curtains hung down from the ceiling to the bed. The balcony window was stained glass. It depicted the goddess of nature raising her hand in the air. Frieda walked Persela to her bed and sat with her. Frieda reached over with her own gown and whipped Persela's make up off.

"Don't be afraid to call if you need anything," Frieda said before leaving.

Alone again, Persela sat on the edge of the bed and looked down at her hands. She thought back to what happened that night. The incident haunted her. No matter how hard she tried, she could not get the memory to disappear. She stretched her arms around her chest and tried comforting herself. She fell back and lay on the bed. Tears poured out her eyes.

That morning, she didn't bother to get out of bed. A maid walked in and opened the curtains. A ray of light landed on her bedside. Persela hid under the sheets and turned away.

"You should join us for breakfast," the maid politely insisted. Persela didn't respond. Another maid came later that day. "Lunch is ready." Persela did not move. Near the end of the day, a maid stood behind her door and gently knocked. "Dinner," the maid whispered.

Persela turned to face the window near the end of the day. She wanted to watch as the world sunk back into darkness. Someone knocked on her door.

"My dear," Frieda said entering her room. Walking towards the window, she closed them as well as the curtains. She sat on her bedside for some time before getting up. "Sweet dreams my darling," Frieda said walking out.

The next morning no one bothered to come in and open her window. Frieda nor anyone from the house bothered to invite her to breakfast, lunch, or dinner. She laid there, motionless. A world she once knew so bright and warm was now horrifying. And the only thing that once brought her joy now brought her sorrow. She tried searching for another source of happiness but no matter where she searched, Anthony always appeared. *Did he ever really love me?* she wondered. The one person that once filled her world with bliss now filled it was disgust. She tossed in agony wondered, *what now.*

"What a beautiful day," Leo said entering her room the next morning. "I love watching the sunrise." He walked towards the

189

balcony and opened the curtains before sitting on the edge of her bed. Persela naturally turned over and hid under the sheets. "Seriously, I want you to watch the sunrise with me." Leo looked over at the lump of sheets that was Persela. "Come on. At least turn around and take a peak." The sheets moved. Two fingers gently reached from under the silk covers and made a slot for Persela's brown eyes to look through.

"Hmm," was all she could say about the sunrise.

"I can't say I know what you're going through or that I know what it's like." Leo paused to look back at the sunrise. "But what I can tell you is that you are not alone. And what I mean is that, you are not the only one hurting. We are all hurting inside," Leo paused to rub his hands together. Persela looked at the leather gloves that covered his badly scarred hands and wondered what had hurt him. "And the world isn't so bad when you're hurting together."

Chapter XXIV

Persela awoke to the sound of someone trying to sing. She opened her eyes and saw Leo walking through a door then exiting again. He looked like he was looking for something as he walked into another door. Stepping out he looked more relieved. It was a tie. He wrapped it around his neck and began to tie it. Persela got up, Leo looked over at her.

"I'm sorry. I didn't mean to wake you," Leo said edgily. "I have a bad habit of leaving things everywhere and not remembering where I left them."

"What's it doing here and not in your wardrobe?" Persela asked. Leo laughed.

"Believe it or not, I don't really have a room or a wardrobe. Actually, I don't have a room of my own. I sleep in whatever room isn't occupied."

"Were you singing?" Persela asked thinking back to the voice.

"Yea," Leo replied embarrassed.

"Oh," Persela said wanting to laugh but managed to restrain herself.

"Anyways, you should have breakfast this morning."

"You trust me in your home? You're not worried I'll rob you?" Persela asked in a much cheerier mood than the past couple days.

"Yea, I'm not much of the materialistic person," Leo said laughing. Persela stopped and looked at Leo really confused.

"Then why the large house and stuff?"

"I think I did it to provide a sense of security. But to me, it's been nothing but a cage made of gold. A cage nonetheless." Leo said struggling with his tie.

"You need a mirror?"

"Even with a mirror. I was never really good at this."

"Oh, so where you going exactly?" Persela asked.

"I am headed downstairs to the back where I hold an annual event. I would have invited you, but I did not expect you up till later today. God knows how long you teenagers sleep."

"Oh, so you weren't leaving your house at all," Persela said now realizing why he was not worried about being robbed.

"Do you want to come?" Leo said seriously. Persela was stunned, not knowing the proper way of accepting his invitation. She looked down, realizing she was still naked.

"I have nothing to wear," she said slapping her hands on her ruined face. Leo ran his hands down his white suit as he walked through the door he found his tie. He came back with a white dress and handed it to Persela. It was a white crochet summer dress with magnificent flower patterns all over.

"Do you like it? It's pretty warm today. Especially for February."

"I. I. Love it. I've never seen anything like it," Persela said.

"The shower is over there," Leo said pointing at the same door he had been coming from. Someone passed by Persela's room.

"Rosy!" Leo called out. An elderly woman walked in and bowed her head.

"Yes," Rosy said.

"Please help Persela," Leo said in Mandarin. Standing up, he stormed out without saying another word.

———

Persela stepped out and into a magical garden with her new dress. She couldn't help but constantly look down and admire it. It fit perfectly around her body. She loved the way it tightly wrapped around her breasts and waist but hung freely down her knees. She stood by the door looking out into the botanical garden. Seeing all the men and women, she felt out of place and thought about returning to her room.

"Where do you think you're going?" Leo said appearing in front of her. "So, what do you plan on doing after graduating," Leo asked.

"I don't know," Persela said. "So, it seems whatever you planned after college worked out?"

"I didn't go to college," Leo said with a smirk.

"Oh," was all Persela said but inside she was in complete shock. "So, what do you do?"

"What?"

"What do you do," Persela asked again. Persela noticed his gloves as he ran his hands down his white suite. "Show time," he said walking out.

Leo walked out shaking every hand he came across and reached out to those that did not. Going down the crowd of people, he came across a woman. He paused in front of her. Tenderly grabbing her hand, he raised it towards his lips. Kissing her hand, the woman smiled and slightly blushed. So, did Persela witnessing the scene. Leo recognized someone over his shoulder and quickly released the woman's hand. He slapped his hands on his sides and stood up straight. Pivoting like a soldier, he saluted the man behind him. Noticing an elderly white woman standing next to the man, Leo took a knee and placed his right arm across his chest. The elderly woman reached over and patted Leo on his shoulder. Rising to his feet, he bowed at the elderly woman before hugging the man affectionately. Releasing him, they both laughed like old friends. Leo bowed one last time before excusing himself to welcoming everyone else. He was shaking the hand of a man with a handlebar mustache when an Indian couple approached him from behind. The man's ruby red sherwani and the woman's saree made them look glamorous and royal. Leo turned around. He tilted his head and putting his hands together, he bowed respectfully to them. The couple did not bow. Instead, they waited for him to raise his head before they reached their arms over his shoulder and embraced him with a warm hug. He did the same not surprised by their actions. There was not a person there that did not approach Leo. He was comfortable with everyone not afraid to embrace their customs. He spoke their languages and tried his best to welcome everyone to his home.

After it was all done, Leo found Persela and sat down; he ordered a servant to bring a glass of water.

"Wow, you know a lot of people."

"Yea, I guess," Leo said looking around. He looked left, right, and behind Persela. He looked all around until they received their drinks.

"So, what's all this about?"

"It's business really. You invite a lot of important people, and they invite other important people, and they invite their friends. And so on. Business tactic. Politics and all that stuff. This isn't even the best part." Leo looked around again. "Wait till the spring equinox. That's when the real party happens."

"Are you expecting someone?" Persela asked also looking around.

"No, just making sure I did," Leo stopped as his face turned white. Persela looked behind her. She saw a woman admiring the flowers. She had dark skin. Her thick black wavy hair hung down naturally and freely. She had on a red dress that fit tightly around her body. "I'll. I'll. I'll be right back," Leo stuttered keeping his eyes on the woman.

Walking up to the woman, he spoke with a shaky voice. "It's a pleasure seeing you again."

"Umm, I'm sorry I don't know if we've met before," she said brushing her hair from her face and placing it behind her ear.

"Is there anything I can get you, Master Leo?" asked a server passing through.

"Some water. Is that fine with you?" Leo said keeping his eyes on the woman. She nodded in agreement.

"Gladly," the servant replied as he left.

"So, have we ever met before?" she said smiling yet feeling ashamed, not able to remember where she had met Leo before.

"I'm Leo," Leo said feeling his heart jumping around his rib cage.

"Leo! Yes. I'm so sorry for not recognizing you! It's a pleasure to finally meet you, Leo. I've heard so much about you and your grand party. You have a wonderful house and a splendid yard. I felt like a young girl again walking around your garden. I hope you don't mind. I feel so rude being so antisocial but your home…"

"No. No. It's fine," Leo said.

"Leo, how have you been?" Governor Robert said stretching his hand out. Leo jerked, agitated at his intrusion.

"I'm great," Leo said turning to face Robert. Reaching out his hand, they shook hands.

"And who is this beautiful woman?" Robert said looking over. "You should introduce me, Leo," Robert said grinning.

195

"I'm so sorry. I'm Ovella," Ovella said shaking Leo's and Robert's hand.

"Ovella, what a beautiful name. Don't you think, Leo?" Robert said. Leo nodded his head in agreement. The server returned with the glasses of water.

"Oh, come now, Leo. Let's get something worth drinking. Please get us some wine. You don't mind do you, Leo?"

"No, not at all," Leo responded. Once again, the server left. Robert returned his attention to Ovella, who was sipping the glass of water.

"Ovella, what is it that you do?"

"I'm sorry, but I forgot a have to make an important phone call," Leo said.

"Tell Clairis I said hello," Robert said. Leo replied with a half-smile and left. Robert smiled back. Leo calmly walked away and made his way through the crowd. He walked straight to the kitchen and stood there trying to figure out what had just happened. He looked out the window and watched everyone enjoying their time in his home. He was ready to walk back out when Persela walked in.

"You look nervous, she's pretty. You know you don't come off as the shy kinda guy. I'm kinda surprised you just choked out there," Persela said.

"Yea you think so?"

"Yea, you should take a shot. Take the edge off," Persela said. Leo laughed.

"Did you ever have that drink I gave you," Leo asked.

"At the bar?" Persela asked.

"Yea?"

"No, why?"

"You should have. You know it was water, right?"

196

"Are you serious? You know I'm not even mad about that. What upset me more was how you were playing your little mind games on me. That was not cool."

"I'm so sorry. I had to. You thought you were so pretty and irresistible. I thought it be funny to ruin your night."

"And you did! You know I thought about that night for weeks. I really did!"

"Weeks?"

"Yea! So, it was water. But did you leave that shot for me or had you forgotten about it."

"No I got it for you. I just wasn't gonna tell you. I didn't want to build your ego." Feeling the pressure fade away, Leo was ready to walk back out when the kitchen door opened. Ovella stormed inside.

"Have we met before?" Ovella asked quickly. She had a disturbed look on her face. As she waited for Leo to respond, she studied his face. Leo was stunned being approached so aggressively. He was unprepared and was completely caught off guard. Ovella looked down at his gloves.

"Take them off!" Ovella demanded. "I said take them off!" Persela jumped at her demanding tone. She wanted to leave but everything was happening so fast she found herself caught in the middle. Ovella grabbed his hands and removed the gloves that covered his hideous scars. His palms were soft and tender, no longer the hands of a man who had a labor job. She turned them over, her lips trembled at what she found. She recognized the scars that ran above both his knuckles. She looked up at Leo.

"Alejandro?" Leo looked back at her not knowing what to say or do. Ovella released his hands and reached towards his face. She softly placed her hands on his cheeks and ran them down to his chin. "Is that you?" Leo wanted to answer. He wanted to say yes. "You disappeared. No calls, letters, emails, nothing," Ovella whimpered. She removed her right hand and struck Leo's face. His cheek turned red.

Persela snapped and now found the ability to leave in fear she was now interrupting something personal. Ovella looked at Leo with furious yet tender eyes. "Where did you disappear to? What happened?" Ovella continued to ask questions not giving Leo an opportunity to answer. "What happened? You just left."

"Can we sit?" Leo suggested. A servant passed through. "Make sure everyone's drinks are filled and bring us some water as well." Leo pulled up a chair for Ovella and him. Ovella looked for the man she once knew as Alejandro.

"Master Leo," the servant said returning with the drinks.

"Thank you," he said not breaking eye contact from Ovella. "Please attend to the guests and make sure they are enjoying their time. And do me a grand favor. Close the kitchen from anyone to enter. Have the band start playing." He handed her the glass of water. She looked at him deeply. Past the white suit, his new linguistic pattern, and gentlemanly nature, the Alejandro she once knew was still there.

"Master Leo?" Ovella said mocking him. He stared down at the floor embarrassed being called Alejandro again. It was a name that reminded him of someone scared, weak, poor, and useless. "How have you been, Ovella?" Leo asked kindly waiting for his embarrassment to pass.

"Alejandro," Ovella said firmly when someone entered the kitchen. Leo looked over Ovella's shoulder to see who it was. He had deep ocean blue eyes and a menacing look on his face. His blonde hair was uncombed and wild. He looked a mess and as he pointed a gun at Leo, he grated his teeth like a wild beast. Leo looked at the intruder with the same eyes he gave him before. Ovella turned around and jumped up at the sight of a gun. Then her ears started ringing. She looked back at Leo. He placed his hand on his chest and grabbed something from his suit. Something red was oozing out. Just as the ringing in her ears began settling down, Leo slowly fell like a statue crumbling to pieces.

Chapter XXV

Leo woke up to a beeping noise. He noticed it was coming from a machine. He looked over. Persela was resting her head next to his hand. He looked down at all the wires crawling out the white sheets he was under and the machines they were plugged into. Persela woke up feeling his arm moving.

"I'm so sorry, this is all my fault," Persela said crying. Tears ran down her cheeks. Leo was ready to explain that is wasn't her fault when a doctor walked inside and asked her to leave. A nurse stepped in next holding a clipboard and was glancing through a file of papers. She occasionally looked at Leo in disbelief. Finally, she placed the clipboard on the bed and stood next to the doctor.

"Comfortable," asked the doctor.

"Yea," Leo replied.

"Good, I don't know how to word this without having to put any kind of tension in your heart," the doctor started. Leo wondered if he was hinting at something. The doctor sucked his teeth before continuing. "So, you came into my hospital barely alive. Quickly seeing where the bullet punctured you, I had no choice but to go into surgery. To remove the bullet and see if any serious injuries were done. I am sorry to say we remove part of the bullet," the doctor paused seeing a face of confusion on Leo's face. The doctor wanted Leo to feel secure so he continued, "The bullet entered your body and punctured your interventricular septum," Leo tried listening, but as hard as he tried, he had no idea what the doctor was talking about. "We checked your INR," Leo stared up at the ceiling not knowing what an INR and ignored everything else the doctor had to say. "There are parts still that we could not retrieve without damaging your heart. You are very lucky to be alive." He studied Leo and waited for some kind of expression to appear. Leo reached over and placed his hand on his chest. He felt his heartbeat. He chuckled at the idea that it would no longer feel empty. With nothing more to say, the doctor left, leaving Leo to himself.

The next day he was visited by an old friend. He was comfortably sleeping when he woke to someone smacking a book on his forehead. Ms. Emerson stood looking down at Leo. Seeing his eyes open, she sat down.

"I found this little journal of yours in your study room," she waved it around before resting it on her lap. "You have a funny way of getting the past come to you. I thought I told you to leave it," she said.

"I did," Leo snapped.

"No, no, no, don't. Don't cut me off. I don't care who you are. I'll get back up and beat you with this book," Ms. Emerson said waving the book in the air. Leo looked up and realized it was his journal. Ms. Emerson opened it and pulled out a picture. It was an old picture of Leo carrying Ovella on his back. They were both smiling. "I don't know how you pulled out this little stunt but if I find out all this was you're doing, expect consequences."

"Don't you dare touch her," Leo threatened Ms. Emerson.

"I told you clearly to leave the past in the past and what do you do. I know you had Phillip track down your family, and I know you have him watch over them. How do I know he didn't do the same for this girl? I told you, leave the past in the past and what do you do?"

"And I did!"

"Anyways, here's a little something I got you to help you move on," Ms. Emerson said with a smirk. She pulled out another picture from her purse and handed it to Leo. He turned it on its back realizing it was a portrait of Ovella and another man. Both holding on to a new born baby. He felt a sharp pain in his chest. He blamed the bullet lodged in his heart.

"Hmm," was all Leo could say.

"You should have seen their wedding," Ms. Emerson said venomously as Leo folded the photo. "Leo, if I had known all this was for a girl, I don't think I would have given you the opportunity. Let's make this clear. No, let's just have a gentle reminder. Leave the past in the past." She paused to think for a minute.

"I did," Leo said.

"Leo, we are all born for a reason, good or bad. And, well, love is something you don't understand. You don't know how to love someone. It's not in your nature. You're more likely to slice someone's throat. War, chaos, and all that, now that's in your nature. Trust me. I know. I've seen it," Ms. Emerson said getting up. "You have to risk everything for love. You never did. Not with Delilah, Ovella, or Clairis!" She retrieved the family portrait.

"How do I even know this picture is real?"

"Because I met with her." She could tell he wasn't convinced. "I did and I told her who you really are. And not the person you thought you were. Not the writer. Not the construction worker. Not the dreamer. Not the lover. Leo when I found you. You were lost. You didn't know who you were. Admit it." Leo looked away disgusted at what Ms. Emerson was telling him. "I know who you truly are and I know that you can't love. You couldn't love Beatrice when you were given another chance. Even after you found out she was sick. You were still afraid to love her. Too busy trying to become an honest man. Leo, an honest man?" Ms. Emerson laughed.

"Leave," Leo said hearing Beatrice's name.

"But you risked your life killing Nico and his father. You risked coming to America. You risked your life for me. You risked burning down the world. Leo, be honest with yourself. You're a monster."

"Leave!"

"Remember what I said all those years ago. Leave the past because it can misguide you from the present and never dream of the future as it can prolong what you are destined to be. Accept who you are Leo," was all Ms. Emerson said as she handed over the black journal.

Ms. Emerson never visited again, but Persela's constantly did. Leo admitted her visitations were always a delight. Persela felt a sense of debt to Leo after what happened. She wanted to care for him the way he had cared for her. He had been so welcoming from the moment they met, and now was her chance to repay him or, at least, care for him the best she could. She always asked him if he was comfortable, if he needed anything, or if there was anything she could do to make his stay more pleasing. So, when Leo mentioned how he hated the hospital meals and craved a simple peanut butter sandwich, Persela knew what had to be done.

"Crust or no crust?" she asked.

"Does it matter really?"

"Yea, it kinda does. I want you to enjoy the sandwiches I make you. So, crust or no crust?" Persela asked again.

"No crust, I guess."

"What do you mean you guess?" Persela asked giggling.

"I've never been asked that question," Leo said scratching the back of his head.

"Ok. Ok. No crust," she said looking at Leo with a childish smile.

After weeks of recovering, Leo was finally ready to leave. Persela was glad but at the same time disappointed that she was no longer going to be caring for Leo. She hesitated when she handed him a new suit that Frieda had given her for Leo.

"Are you sure Leo. You should stay a day or more.," Persela constantly asked him.

"I'm ready," Leo insisted. "I have another event that I can't miss." Handing over the outfit, Leo stepped into a changing room. Inside, he buttoned up his shirt then looked in the mirror. He stopped to look at his reflection. He reached over and placed his finger on his chest where they had done open chest surgery. A large scar ran vertically in the middle of his chest. He was disgusted with it and with the scars on his hands. *I'm beginning to look more and more like a beast from hell*, he thought. *I'll never be able to change who I am*, he thought thinking back to what Ms. Emerson said.

"You think too much. You know I don't care about your scars," Beatrice said. Leo tried envisioning her face but couldn't but he could feel her standing next to him just as she would every time he put on a button up shirt. Her arms tightly wrapping around him. "I don't care about your past." He could almost feel her head resting on his shoulder. He thought about raising his hand to feel her hair but he knew no one was there. "I don't care about your future," she said. "Stop overthinking so much and just stand by me."

"So, how you feeling?" Persela asked stepping into the limo. Leo's chauffeur closed the door behind them. "Are you sure you should be coming home so early? You know I don't mind watching over you. Seriously."

"No, I'm fine," Leo said rolling his window down. He looked out at the passing pedestrians and seemed to be transfixed on them. Persela watched him as he studied everyone that passed. She wondered what he was thinking. She remembered when she first met him at the bar. He was staring off into space just like he was doing now. The limousine stopped at a red light. Persela heard music approaching. A

203

green truck stopped next to them. The man driving was wearing a hard hat that had a Mexican flag sticker on it. The passenger had on a baseball cap. Their faces were covered in grease and dirt.

"I never liked that kind of music," she said expecting Leo to agree. She looked over and unexpectedly saw him mouthing the lyrics. As the truck vanished and the music faded, Leo continued singing. Persela blushed having insulted Leo. She looked away and tried thinking of something to say. She thought about apologizing then looked back at Leo.

"Are you Mexican?" Persela said.

"Yea," Leo said still staring out the window.

"Oh, I'm sorry. I didn't know."

"I mean, I was born in Mexico, but I was also born in a place called Earth." Persela had nothing to say. "So, you've been visiting me a lot. What are your professors going to think?"

"I don't care really. Honestly, I don't think I'm going back," Persela said. Leo thought he understood why. So, he did not blame her or question her decision.

"So, what are you?" Leo asked returning to the previous topic.

"Like race? Honestly, I don't know. Both my parents were adopted."

"Oh, aren't you lucky. You can be whoever," Leo said. "What if you were Mexican?" Leo suggesting with his large smile.

"What if I was?" Persela said gasping and widening her eyes. They looked at each other thinking of the possibility.

"Maybe Puerto Rican?" Leo suggested.

"No, I'm not pretty enough," Persela teased. "Brazilian," she said brushing her hair sexually.

"We'll find out," Leo said turning his attention back to the passing people.

"What?" Persela said confused.

"I know I'm a week behind but every year since I bought my estate, on March 20 we have a celebration. I invite everyone who resides at my palace to bring their family to my home. I don't know if you noticed but my house if filled with people from all over the world."

"Why March 20?" Persela asked.

"March 20th is typically when we have the spring equinox. That's when night and day are about the same. It's when light finally wins." Persela tried to envision the event, but nothing would come close to what was planned for her. How could she imagine all the colors, languages, food, music, and cultural from every region of the world if she had never once traveled away from her home country.

Leo returned to his estate surprised by the number of people already present. The house lit up in excitement at Leo's arrival. Everyone stormed the kitchen to prepare a feast before nightfall. Persela tried her best to fit in but was overwhelmed by the number of different languages. Every tongue from all parts of the world could be heard roaming under his roof. Erotic smells quickly traveled from the kitchen and into the corridors and every bedroom in the palace. Leo's estate was so brightly lit with different colors of clothing. Children chased one another throughout the hallways and stairways. Leo smiled at all the children and at the people.

———

"Frieda, I need you to do something for me," Leo said desperately.

"What is it, Leo?" she asked concerned. Leo said nothing as she followed him to the third floor. Once inside he pulled a black leather journal out.

"I want you to take this," Leo said. He placed it on top of a stack of books then pulled out a gold wax seal with the infinity symbol on it.

"My dear, Leo, what's going on?" Frieda asked concerned with Leo's mysterious behavior. Burning the wax, Leo sealed his journal. He stumbled across some books and reached down to grab a knife. Firmly, he inscribed the words, "beyond the good and evil," on it. Frieda wondered what the phrase meant when Leo handed him his journal.

"I need her to know who I am. Ms. Emerson told her, but it's not all true. I need her to know that I tried. I need her to know that I'm not a monster. That everything I did was out of love." Leo said on edge. He handed Frieda a note with Ovella's name and address. "I can't do it because I know she's watching."

As the sun was setting, a crowd of people gathered around a fire deep inside the botanical garden. A group of musicians started tuning their instrument. A soft folk tune started playing. Persela stood amid all the excitement when Leo yelled, "Pizzica!" Persela jumped, startled by his announcement. Leo grabbed Persela's hand and guided her to the center of the crowd.

"I hope you like to dance," Leo said with an intimidating smirk.

"Dance what?" Persela replied.

"Pizzica."

"I don't even know what that is," Persela said scared. *Is he serious*, she wondered as the music started to come together. Leo raised his arms and started clapping his hands in beat with the music, others followed behind him. The musicians then stopped, but the clapping continued. They discussed among themselves and came to an agreement on what song to play. Leo and everyone continued clapping. Someone yelled in a different language. A little girl ran towards Persela and handed her a red scarf. An accordion started. Everyone stopped clapping. Persela quickly grew excited and scared at the same time as a guitar followed with a soft entrance. Everyone started clapping in excitement, chanting, and yelling. Finally, an elderly woman started singing as the violinist sped the tempo. A handsome young woman entered the center and began to dance. She stopped to look into the crowd and, raising her hand, she pointed at someone within the crowd. Persela looked in the direction she was pointing. It was a man. She lowered her hand and began rocking her hips side to side. Slowly, following the rhythm of the music, the man walked to the center of the circle. The man began dancing around her as she continued to rock her hips. Persela looked at the woman studying her moves and noticed she was holding on to a red scarf, just like the one she was given. She wondered if having the scarf was a good thing and if she was going to have to dance. Persela watched as the woman and man danced pizzica. It was majestic and energetic in a completely different way. She could not help but smile at the idea of being part of it.

"Wish me luck," Leo said biting his lower lip.

"Oh, my God! What are you about to do?" Persela nervously shouted in excitement. She covered her blushing face as Leo danced his way to the center. "Oh, my God, please don't trip," she said afraid. Leo raised one hand in the air and placed the other on his waist. He approached the woman. She also raised one hand in the air and approached Leo, her red scarf dangling in the air. Their hands never touched but their eyes locked into each other. Leo calmly reached over to grab the scarf and tangled their hands together. Locking their eyes and hands together, they began to spin slowly. The music sped up and so did their spinning. The woman untangled her hand from the scarf and released Leo. Leo took a knee and stretched his hands out. She began spinning faster and faster inside Leo's arm. The music suddenly stopped, everyone yelled and clapped in joy. Leo smiled in agreement. As he stood up, the woman handed the scarf over to Leo.

"You have pinched my heart," she said in poor English. Leo smiled like a child.

"Leo!" Persela shouted in excitement. "Why didn't she want her scarf anymore?"

"At the end of the dance, the woman gives her scarf to the man who's won her heart," Leo said out of breath. "Beautiful, isn't it?"

Leo looked at the scarf, examining it as if there was something hidden. Turning to Persela, he admitted, "This is my first time being chosen!" Leo looked around. Everyone was silent as they waited for the next performance. "Not surprised. There always late. I'll be right back."

"Um, ok." Persela watched as Leo disappeared into the crowd. Turning towards the crowd, she stood on her toes, anticipating the next show. No one appeared. She glanced back to see if Leo was returning. He was not. Instead, she was face to face with a young brown-skinned girl with a curly afro.

"Hello," said the stranger.

"Hi," Persela responded.

"Did shu dense Pizzica?"

"Dense? Oh dance. No, but Leo did."

"Yes, dance." She smiled. "Leo! Good. I love pizzica. I love music. Me and my friend." She looked around. "Wherever she is."

"Where are you from?" Persela asked. Interested in her accent, she grew curious. "I'm so sorry. I'm Persela. What's your name?" The girl just smile.

"Marebel, I am from Cuba, but my grandparents are from Africa."

"There you are!" Leo said returning with a girl. "My two Yoruba Queens are next."

"Ah, you found Bella," Marebel said excited.

"You two are a handful every year," Leo said smiling.

"Handful?" Bella asked as Marebel grabbed her hand and led her to the middle of the crowd.

The crowd broke out in excitement seeing the two enter the center. They bowed and thanked everyone for their patience. The crowd grew silent. Persela anxiously watched them. When they finally began, everyone was awestruck. They had a gentle yet powerful voice.

208

Their voice was sweet and soulful to Persela's ears and even though she did not know their language, Persela could feel the passion and sorrow behind it. When it was over. Persela felt like she was traveling through the world. Starting in Italy with pizzica, making their way through Europe they went south to Africa. From there she went East, all the way to Asia. She watched as every culture was expressed. Leo insisted on joining in the fun with every culture. Although she continually refused, she did finally join the belly dancers. She was an amateur compared to the rest, but no one judged her. They all applauded after the dance. Finally, as Persela thought the night was coming to an end, a large mariachi group approached the center. Everyone whistled, yelled, and clapped their hands together as the mariachi group bowed. Picking up their instruments a woman in a beautiful orange dress appeared. The music quickly started as the woman twirled in circles, swirling her dress around. Leo whistled in excitement then let out a yell of excitement. Persela giggled, seeing Leo so ecstatic. Not being able to restrain himself, Leo danced by himself the entire song.

"Teach me how to dance," Persela asked when it was over.

"Yea, why not?" Leo said out of breath.

A cool breeze blew over Persela's shoulder and into Leo's face. Tree branches swayed as the morning sun made its way up from the ground. A chill ran up Persela's spine. She did not know if it was the wind or the way Leo placed his hands on her side but she could not help but look at him shyly. She felt thirteen again, afraid of boys. She looked down at her feet and then back at him.

"Don't be nervous," Leo said. Music started; it was the same song Persela had heard coming from the green truck. "You look great by the way," Leo said praising her summer dress. "Ok, follow my lead." He stepped side to side. She did the same trying to keep up but felt awkward the entire song. Leo could tell she was uncomfortable and was not embarrassed to tell the band to stop.

"Let's try something else," Leo said. Another song came up. "I think you'll enjoy this more." He released her to remove his gloves. "I'm sorry. If you feel uncomfortable, I can put them back on."

"No," Persela insisted.

"Ok," Leo said placing his left hand on her hip and wrapped his right hand with hers. Her heart skipped a beat. With their fingers wrapped around each other, she felt his soft palm up against hers and the scar tissue on the other side.

"Play a simple rhythm," Leo said to the band. The band spoke to one another before deciding what to play next.

"Ok," she said out of breath. She had never been so close to someone before. She wanted the moment to last. She wanted to be held with care and love and never be let go. She embraced him and let go all her fears.

"Yea you got it." Leo moved her gently, guiding her hips properly with his hand. He tried his best to hold her gently yet firmly around his arm as if trying to tell her that he would never let go. She stepped on his foot. "It's ok," Leo insisted. She bit her lower lip. He wanted to kiss her lips every time she did that.

"Oh, I'm sorry," Persela said stepping on his foot again. Leo could not help but adore Persela's clumsiness.

"You got it," Leo said releasing her hip and gently spinning her. Returning her to his arms, Leo wrapped his arm around her waist. They were tightly close to each other. His heart exploded. His stomach quickly got warm. He instantly became happy. A smile appeared on his face as he pressed his body closer to hers. His heart began to beat uncontrollably. Leo looked down at Persela, who was looking up at him. A set of words rested heavy on his lips. The song ended as he quickly released her. "I'm sorry. I don't feel well," Leo said as he walked away. "You're welcome to stay in your room," was the last thing he said as he disappeared into the botanical garden.

———

Inside his botanical garden, Leo was sitting down on a bench when Philip arrived. "You been here for a while?" Philip asked.

"Yea, since morning," Leo replied.

"You should think about getting some rest. You just got back from the hospital."

"I'll think about it," Leo said.

"You know how I hate hospitals, right?" Philip said.

"Let's walk," Leo suggested. They got up and walked down a red brick trail. Leo said nothing for a while.

Philip could tell he was deep in thought. *I fucked up this time,* he thought.

"Yea, I didn't expect to see you," Leo said.

"Yea."

"So, do tell," Leo turned to look at a bird landing on a tree. "What happened?"

"Well after you got shot Frieda made sure no one found out. She didn't want to scare your guests. She got your chauffeur to drive you the hospital."

"Did anyone ask about my absence?"

"Luckily, no. And because we didn't' want to make a big scene. We had to let the kid get away."

"So, who's the kid?" Leo said looking back at Philip.

"I don't know how your gonna feel about this."

"I don't have all day, Philip," Leo snapped. "How the fuck did he get into my house? Who let the little shit in? At least, tell me that!" Philip didn't say anything. "Who's the kid who shot me?" Leo shouted.

"It's Robert's kid," Philip started. Leo's half smile appeared. "The plan was to hand over The Pool Table Club. You know the one that in his school. Yea, hand it over to his son, Anthony. He's not that

211

bright. Real egotistical, power hungry, narcissistic, not that bright kind of person. Not like his father. Have him make some mistakes. Spend dirty money here and there then tie Robert into everything and you know where we go from there." Leo's mouth opened as he tried speaking. "He managed to get into your house because our guards knew who he was. Who his father was. They thought he was a guest."

"I," Leo stopped. "I think I should shoot you just to be fair," he said. Philip's face went pale. "I'm not, though. Ok, this is what we're going to do. I just wanted to have dirt on Robert, but now I want you to ruin Robert's career and kill his only son." Leo looked straight into Philip's eyes, "I'm serious. Kill his kid and ruin Robert's career. I want him to suffer! And! I want you to burn everyone in that club. Literally burn them all alive inside that house and afterward, when everyone shows up, I want all the money tying back to Robert. I want the whole press on his ass. I want him to live. Yea, Robert needs to live. I want him to suffer through a tarnished career."

"Sounds like a good plan. What about the girl? Are you sure she doesn't know too much?"

"No, I'm sure. Let's pretend she doesn't exist," Leo looked at Philip who was wondering if he was being dismissed. "Sometimes I wonder if all the things I've done are one day going to come back and haunt me."

"Well, just try not to think about it."

"Then I stop and wonder. Everyone I've done harm to. I'm almost sure that when I die and go to hell, when I look both ways, they'll be sitting next to me."

"Hmm," was all Philip said as they reached Beatrice's gravestone.

"You're free to go," Leo said. He leaned against the cold marble thinking, regretting.

Chapter XXVI

The next morning, Persela was awakened by Frieda handing her a note. It was from Leo apologizing and explaining he had an urgent business trip. He had left first thing that morning. She knew, or thought she knew, he had no business trip. She felt stupid, not knowing why.

"Leo is afraid of a lot of things," Frieda said gently on Persela's bedside. "Love being one of them." Persela noticed a disappointed look on Frieda's face. "He refuses to forgive himself of someone he once was but isn't anymore. You're more than welcome to stay as long as you want. But I know you have a life other than this. Whenever you're ready, I can have someone drive you back to school."

"I think I'm ready to go," Persela said.

"I'll fetch our driver," Frieda said getting up.

"Tell Leo something for me," Persela started.

"Yes, dear?"

"Tell him that everyone is suffering and that he shouldn't have to suffer alone. Tell him the world isn't so bad when we suffer together."

Persela stood on the street curb staring at her university. She was afraid to step foot on campus. She couldn't go back to a factitious world. She wanted something real. That's when she thought of Marc. She turned around and made her way to the nearest bus stop.

He was inside packing a suitcase when she entered. She stood there watching him for a while not knowing what to say or what to do.

"Umm, so where you going," she asked fixing her hair. He turned around and looked at her. He had a small smile on his face.

"I thought you disappeared on me."

"No, just been under the weather. So, where you going?"

"I'm leaving," Marc said throwing a shirt on top his suitcase. He closed it then sat on the floor.

"So, what about your paintings?"

"You wanna come with me," Marc asked completely ignoring her question. He looked at her almost afraid of what her answer was going to be. "I'll gladly leave all my paintings behind if you come."

"You don't want me. I'm not all that great. Besides we just barely met." Persela looked down.

"Yea, I do. And I know we just met but it feels real with you." Marc said. He stretched his hand out. "I can't promise you everything. But I can promise you that I won't ever leave your side." Persela looked up at him. She walked towards him and grabbed his hand.

Unknown Date

Last Journal Entry
We are not Gods so love without fear as all mortals should

She told me she was sick but that it was something she'd had since birth. I never thought much about it. I wish I had. Everything was so sudden and before I knew it I was burying her. I didn't cry. I remember feeling angry. Angry at myself. After the funeral, I sat in what felt like an empty apartment with a pencil and paper trying to write for the first time in a long time. I thought that if I wrote about her she would live forever. But nothing ever came. I tried to remember what she looked like but her face was becoming a blur. Scared I tried to recall other things. Her favorite color, a conversation we had, the way she laughed, her birthday, a childhood memory of hers, her birthplace, the elementary school she'd attended, nothing. In the end, I could only remember one thing. A small memory of us.

I'd be staring off into space, regretting my past and worrying about my future. Beatrice knew this. She would walk up behind me, wrap her arms around my waist, then rest her head on my shoulder.

"You think too much. You know I don't care about your scars. I don't care about your past. I don't care about your future. Stop overthinking so much and just stand by me. You and I are here for such a short time, so love as much as you can without fear."

About the Author

Francisco Dosal has been interested in different form of arts since childhood. He brings his creative energy to bear as a writer, an oil painter, a photographer, and an entrepreneur. Mr. Dosal resides in the Atlanta metro area where he is proudly partnered with LowKii Board Co., an up and coming skateboard and street attire company serving the skateboarding community.